What the critics are saying:

Five Stars from Just Erotic Romance Reviews
"This story showcases Lorie O'Clare's incredible writing talents and is sure to be a favorite among werewolf lovers."

"I definitely recommend this sexy, action-packed story to everyone." *-Enya Adrian, Romance Reviews Today*

LUNEWULF 2: IN HER BLOOD
n Ellora's Cave Publication, July 2004

Ellora's Cave Publishing, Inc.
PO Box 787
Hudson, OH 44236-0787

ISBN #1-84360-898-7

ISBN MS Reader (LIT) ISBN # 1-84360-677-1
Other available formats (no ISBNs are assigned):
Adobe (PDF), Rocketbook (RB), Mobipocket (PRC) & HTML

Edited by *Delyn Eagling*
Cover art by *Darrell King*

LUNEWULF 2: IN HER BLOOD

Lorie O'Clare

Chapter One

Elsa watched through unblinking eyes as the buck strolled into the clearing. She sat on her hind legs. Her fur-covered bottom resting against the crushed pine needles and rough twigs that covered the forest floor. The stillness around her fueled her predatory desires. Nothing moved.

She tensed, preparing herself for the kill. This was what she had been waiting for. This moment. This hunt. The battle between her and her meal.

Her eyes narrowed as the buck's head lifted, his nostrils flaring, body tensing as he tested the air. She knew the moment he sensed her. The rigidness of his large body, the scent of his sweat, his fear.

Her mouth watered from the pungent aroma, the need to lick her lips overwhelming her. She wanted to taste his flesh. Feel his warm blood trickling down her throat. The thrill of meat well earned.

Staring at her prey, Elsa's muscles quivered, her heart racing with anticipation. The fear of the buck prevailed and he took flight.

She flew at the large animal, even though he was more than head and shoulders taller than she. His speed and strength were no match to her breed. She was his ultimate executioner. Natural selection, raw and primitive. He screamed in terror, the sound echoing through the night, filling her senses, racing through her blood as she narrowed the distance between them.

The peak moment had arrived.

Her dagger-like claws grabbed on to a thick hind leg and her breath caught at the sensation when she punctured through the hide, like puncturing a grape with her teeth — *POP*.

Danger penetrated the air, strong, powerful, throwing her off balance. She turned, almost stumbling, snarling as the buck broke free. It continued to run, not yet aware of its injuries, but Elsa stilled. She tested the damp air, watching the night carefully, the fur on the back of her neck bristling in fury.

Strutting, confident, he approached her without caution. Fur blacker than night, muscles rippling, a werewolf like none she had seen before. She stood in awe, staring as the magnificent creature approached her.

She had known her share of alpha males, but never one like this. He was so massive. Her skin prickled, tingling sensations rippled across her nerve endings. An overwhelming desire to roll over and offer her belly rushed through her. She hadn't considered spreading her legs for any man, or werewolf, since she'd left home. Now thoughts of this powerful beast mounting her teased her muted desires to distraction.

The scent of fresh blood and raw earth was suddenly replaced by another, more primitive smell. Lust and submission — her submission. It shocked her. The sweet smell of wantonness filled her nostrils, causing her heart to trip in fear. Because she knew he had detected it. Knew he recognized it for what it was.

His muscles twitched. His brown eyes narrowed while he stared, gleaming with carnal intent. He moved through the underbrush, coming closer to her. She knew he wasn't after her kill.

His almond-shaped eyes glowed in surprise for only a moment while Elsa felt the breath slam from her chest. Her heart raced as her body quivered with the sensations that flooded through her.

Deep, forbidding, a low masculine growl rumbled from his powerful chest, resonating with carnal dominance — demanding submission. Elsa trembled at the sound, sexual heat flaring in the pit of her belly at his demand. His mouth opened, white teeth, longer than a man's fingers, flashed through the blackness of the night. A thick, red tongue edged slightly out of his mouth and a wicked grin appeared. Confidence. Arrogance. His certainty that she was his irked her.

She stared at him for a minute before the pain in her chest reminded her to breathe. The sexual tension saturating the air demanded she move and move now. Instinctively, she backed away.

She had two choices. Belly up, or run like hell. She could roll over, spread her legs and offer her sweet juices to this unknown werewolf. She watched as his thick tongue slid over his upper lip, moistening his glossy coat and imagined that rough texture rousing her swollen entrance. She almost went down in the rear thinking about it. She wanted to give her ass a quick shake to prod it back to reality, but didn't dare.

Black as the night, more carnal than sin, he was cloaked with the scent of nature and power. He was one with the darkness — the master of it. He showed no sign of hesitation. He would consume her, take her.

He was so damned big. That cocky strut of his gave proof to the fact that he didn't hear the word "No" that often. She would simply be another piece of tail. That left a sour taste in her mouth. She chose to run like hell.

He would chase her. She wanted him to chase her.

As she turned to flee, she glimpsed his powerful muscles bunch, ripple. His howl rent the air. Challenging. Forceful. Unease rippled down Elsa's back at the meaning of the sound. He was warning not just her, but anyone near. *This bitch is mine!*

The overgrown black and tan brute mistook her petite features as a sign that she couldn't take care of herself. He must have thought since she was petite she was helpless. Were men the same everywhere? She would show this werewolf—this alpha male—that she wasn't his play toy. He might be twice her size, but speed was an asset of her breed. And she was purebred. This American werewolf didn't stand a chance against her *lunewulf* heritage. She couldn't be caught—by anyone. If the wrong person spotted her, it would be all over. They would take her home. And going back wasn't an option.

White as the moon. Rick Bolton had never seen anything like her. Silver eyes, defiant with curiosity, watched him for a mere moment, before she turned and disappeared through the trees. She moved with grace, like a princess.

She'd surprised him, taking on that buck without hesitation. Most bitches hunted smaller animals, or left the hunting to their mates. But this sexy thing enjoyed the attack, the fire in her defiant eyes captivated him at first glance.

She wasn't a bitch from his pack. He'd never se~~en~~ before. If she belonged to one of the other packs i~~n~~ state, she was new to his territory. He would remembered a beautiful white werewolf like Something that beautiful shouldn't be running by herse~~lf~~

Her small body, tempting, slender and pet~~ite~~ distracted him. Her alluring aroma clung to the a~~ir~~ making her trail easy to follow. Tempting and erot~~ic~~ without fear. She moved quickly, not wishing to b~~e~~ captured. That wish could be granted for the moment.

Run for now, moon princess. But you're mine!

Her fluid movements never faltered. Nor did she look back. But she had to know he would follow. Her independence grabbed him, adding to her sensual beauty.

He watched her retreat, stilling his natural impatience, his carnal need for the moonlit bitch that had fled so suddenly. He had been without a woman for months. Without a mate for too long. But that was about to change. This female, who would attack prey twice her size, and not belly up for him, intrigued him. He had to know more about her.

He followed at a careful distance, willing to let her believe she had escaped. For now. Her independence intrigued him. Her glossy white coat mesmerized him.

He paused at the edge of the woods, allowing the darkness to shield him as he watched her approach a deserted vehicle. Her body transformed, white fur turning to long streaming locks. Her coat altering into creamy white skin. Large breasts, a firm tummy, narrow hips, and slender long legs. He would make a feast out of her.

She paused beside the car, comfortable in her nudity, in the isolation of the night. Rick could feel his heart

slamming into his chest as she opened the door, bent… God, that was a view to die for. He could take her, enjoy that perfect body, fuck her until she begged him to do her over and over again.

Her slender legs, tight ass, and narrow waist were partially hidden by her long blonde hair. She slipped into jeans, stretched while she pulled a sweatshirt over her head. Full round breasts silhouetted in the darkness had his paws tingling as he thought of his male hands cupping them. Feeling her nipples harden. Hearing her moan at his touch. Fire burned through him, her perfection making him drool with lust.

This moon princess was in his territory, making her his responsibility. Although his body screamed at him to make his presence known, learn who she was tonight, he knew she would balk from his advances. She hadn't been a solitary bitch looking for a quick fuck on a lonely night, or she wouldn't have run. He didn't know what possessed her to be out, so far from town, and all by herself. But finding out wouldn't be difficult. He had a feeling getting to know her would be a pure pleasure.

He could smell her hesitation. It was a part of their species, the detection of each emotion. Like a sweet, addicting narcotic the scent of her arousal had wrapped around his senses. As had the darker scent of her fear. Just like he knew she had detected his lust.

Amusement rippled through his mind, that and confidence. He wouldn't let her escape as easily as she might believe she had. Their species was unique. Their abilities both human and animal, magnified. He would find her and he would take her. Because he had sensed something more. Something he hadn't seen since his

previous mate had perished in that fire, the awareness that this woman, in all her shining beauty, was meant for him.

Run for now, moon princess. But know you are now protected — and claimed.

Chapter Two

Elsa adjusted her sweatshirt, clothes feeling strange after weeks of being in her fur, and turned nervously. He was watching her. She couldn't prove it, not with her human eyes. But he was out there. And who the hell was he, anyway?

She kept her hand on the car, the cold metal somehow offering sanctuary while she stumbled around and got in on the driver's side. Walking on two legs again seemed awkward.

Smells were all different. Everything was different. She shivered, her fur no longer protecting her sensitive flesh.

"Where are my damned keys?" She needed to quit shaking, to still the racing of her heart. That damned werewolf really shook her up.

Even in her human form, her senses were heightened, a gift her species had. But she dealt now with the limitations of her human senses. Darkness cloaked her ability to see him.

After finding her keys under the mat, Elsa started the car, turned on the headlights, and used the beams to help her see in the dark, searching. He wouldn't have taken off. The fact that he could see her, knew exactly what she was doing, while she didn't have a clue what he did, made her nuts.

"Get an eyeful, mister?" she growled in disgust, wishing she could ignore her pulsing pussy.

She pushed in the clutch, grinding gears. Hell, it'd been a while since she'd driven. The seat slapped her ass while she bounced across the field, toward the road, back into civilization. The small bag, carrying everything she owned, slid off the backseat onto the floor. She reached for it, putting it on the seat next to her. Time to be human again.

Elsa shifted gears, pulling onto the two-lane highway. Thank God no other cars were around to see her drive from the field onto the road. Getting stopped and questioned for parking in the middle of an isolated field would just add to her problems. Right now she needed to figure out a new place to hide.

She gripped the steering wheel, not sure where to go. Her nerves were frazzled.

And that wasn't the only thing. Dampness soaked the crotch of her jeans while her pussy pulsed in beat with her heart. Longing spread through her body. An ache spawning in her womb. She reached down, her fingers rubbing against the swollen lips of her cunt through her jeans, wishing away the pain.

None of this made any sense. Elsa had longed to be fucked before. Needing a man's touch wasn't a new sensation. But something had happened back there in the forest. More than just a stray werewolf interrupting her kill. An attraction stronger than anything she'd experienced before still lingered, pulsing through her veins. He'd compelled her with his raw power, a driving carnal need, his cocky self-assuredness. And she worried his interest in her might be strong enough for him to follow her, track her down.

And you would love it if he found you.

A marquee advertising rooms for rent caught her eye as she drove into the nearby town. Elsa pulled into the gravel parking lot and stared warily at the brightly lit sign. Why were her insides in such a frenzy?

Her taut firm breasts were swollen, heavy and craving to be sucked. The material of her sweatshirt brushed against her nipples, hard and eager to be nibbled on.

"This is ridiculous." She scowled at her behavior, turning off the car. "You can't afford to act this way, Elsa."

Lecturing herself did nothing to calm her rattled nerves. It did nothing to still the heat that was like a virus gone mad throughout her system. Her hands shook while she walked across the parking lot to the small lobby. The last thing she wanted was to spend money on a room for the night. Her funds were limited, and would be until she could access the money her parents had left her.

Elsa tossed her bag on the bed, cringing at the stale smell of the room. At least she could enjoy a hot shower. No man would be impressed with the image staring back at her through the dirty mirror. Pale, too thin, her hair stringy and tangled, right now she'd make the werewolf who had chased her so eagerly in her fur turn and run if he saw her.

But you don't want him to chase you. Remember that.

Elsa stood under the shower, steamy water pelting her skin, massaging life back into her sore muscles. She arched into the warmth of it, then tipped her head back soaking her hair. Almost involuntarily her hands drifted over her body, caressing her breasts, the smooth line of her stomach. Thoughts of the werewolf, so big, and so determined, drifted through her mind.

It bugged her that she wanted him so badly. Her pussy was hot, cum covering her fingers when she parted the soft folds. Her flesh ached for him, but it shouldn't be like this. She shouldn't be coming for a werewolf she didn't even know.

"You don't even know who he is." Great. Now she was talking to herself.

She didn't react like this for any other werewolf who happened to look her way.

Controlling her body and her needs had never been a problem. But something about this werewolf—this man— made her ache to know him better. He had been so confident, so sure of himself as he approached her. It was as if he owned her, and had finally taken time to seek her out.

"But no one owns you, Elsa," she chided herself, jerking her hands back from the velvet heat of her body.

Throttling her frustrated moan, she grabbed the soap and washcloth. She scrubbed her body, enjoying the tingling along her skin, the feel of the lather on her flesh. "You are your own bitch. And you've worked very hard to keep that status," she reminded herself.

She couldn't forget that. Almost three months of running, hiding, continually moving, couldn't end with getting careless over some sexy hunk of a werewolf. She had too much at risk here.

It hadn't been easy, escaping her pack. The law that had been dictated by the pack leader, Elsa's grandmother, provided a damned good reason to run. She was purebred, a *lunewulf*, and her species was endangered.

Grandmother Rousseau had chosen three mates for her. Now, fucking three men didn't sound like a bad thing.

But no one was going to tell her whom to fuck. And she didn't want the three mates who had been chosen for her.

Hiding, covering her tracks, and moving before she got too cozy had kept her free.

Drooling over some gorgeous werewolf could only cause trouble.

Her body wasn't listening to her though.

She turned in the water, propping a foot on the side of the tub, allowing the cascade to hit her burning pussy with pounding force. Tiny droplets vibrated over the tormented flesh while Elsa ran her fingers over her slick cunt, feeling the moist heat, the vibration of the droplets. Desire mingled with the steam in the bathroom.

She wanted to be fucked, needed a cock, thick and hard, thrusting deep inside her. She wanted to experience the raw carnal hunger of that werewolf in the forest. Know his aggression. Experience his confidence. The way those dark brown eyes had devoured her, marking her with his gaze, made her quiver. Lust flooded through her like a hot stream.

"Dammit woman. You are going to get yourself into trouble." She turned off the water, frustrated that she couldn't control the direction of her thoughts.

Toweling dry, she rubbed until heated friction pinkened her skin. She needed to stay focused. She wouldn't be in this room right now if she hadn't gotten careless. That werewolf never should have found her, or been able to follow her.

"You wanted him to follow you, and you know it." She glared at her image in the foggy mirror.

Either way, he did follow her, and more than likely saw the car she was driving. Bad. Bad. Bad. If he had spotted one of the fliers that her pack had put out, then she was history. Somehow, she needed to get out of this town unnoticed and put a lot of miles between her and that distracting werewolf.

Chapter Three

Sleeping on the gravel in the parking lot would have been more comfortable than that motel room bed. Every muscle and joint ached. Elsa swore the damned mattress was stuffed with rocks. And it looked like the only way to get a cup of coffee would be to drive further into town. This day was not starting out well.

"At least in my fur I don't crave caffeine." She tossed her bag onto the backseat. It was that damned werewolf's fault.

Maybe if her dreams hadn't distracted her through the night she would have slept better. The werewolf who had chased her the night before still ransacked her thoughts. She didn't want to think about him anymore, but he wouldn't get out of her mind.

Pulling out of the parking lot, she glanced at the businesses as she drove. A small diner, advertising "All the Ribs You Can Eat on Friday Night", caught her attention. She frowned at a sudden whining sound coming from her engine.

"Please don't die on me now." She stroked the dashboard, fighting the panic that was rising as she realized she could end up stranded. "We've got to stick together, old car."

Getting stuck in this town could be dangerous. A werewolf in the area distracted her dreams, making her crave him when she didn't even know his name.

The temperature gauge soared toward the red just when she pulled into the parking lot. Losing her transportation would also make dodging her pack more difficult. Her heart pounded in her chest while thoughts of being forced home by her pack members settled in her gut like a rock. She would be watched twenty-four/seven to insure she didn't run again. A drop of sweat trickled down between her breasts, her nerves on overdrive. There was no way she could endure that type of existence.

"Looks like we're both overheated." She cursed, and cut the engine.

The diner was almost full of werewolves enjoying breakfast, chatting easily. Holy shit! She'd just walked into the local pack's lair. Rich aromas of fried beef, grease, and strong coffee lingered around them. Her heart pounded like thunder against her chest. She wiped sweaty palms on her jeans. Allowing the door to close behind her, she stood next to the register, terrified to move. But faltering, allowing her fear to show, would alert everyone sitting here that she worried about being seen. They would notice a negative emotion before they noticed the color of her hair. Walking into their pack scared to death would draw even more attention her way.

Most of the tables were full, people chattering while they ate. The werewolf who chased her the night before might be here. She had no idea how he looked as a human. He knew what she looked like though. Curious glances made her uneasy. She had to ignore them though in order to remain calm. Finding a vacant stool by the long counter, she sat.

The waitress approaching focused on the large windows and Elsa followed her gaze, seeing her car outside with the hood up. "Got car trouble?" The young bitch, about the same age as Elsa, had a warm smile. "There's a hose around the side of the building if you need water."

More werewolves than humans filled the booths and tables behind her. The more werewolves who saw her, the better the chances of being recognized from those damned fliers. It wouldn't surprise her if her grandmother had sent them to every pack leader.

"Thanks." She glanced at the menu that the waitress slid in front of her. Her stomach had clenched up in knots. She doubted she would be able to eat now. "I don't need to order any food."

The waitress gave her a curious look when she walked back out of the diner.

Please don't decide to be friendly and follow me. The waitress probably wanted to know why she was traveling alone. *Good little bitches don't run by themselves.* Grandmother's words echoed in her head like a mantra while she walked around the building in search of the hose.

By the time she realized the water hose wasn't long enough to reach the car, and the car wouldn't start to move it closer to the hose, her stomach turned from hunger. She scowled at the morning sun. Her morning had gone from bad to worse before she even had a chance to have coffee.

A blue and white Ford pickup truck parked next to her car. The most gorgeous man she'd seen in quite a while stepped out, walked over to her car, and looked under the hood. She took a step backwards when he straightened, hoping he hadn't noticed her.

It couldn't be…

She broke out in a sweat, the cool shade from the building doing nothing to help. The sensation that she'd met the man she'd just caught a glimpse of before traveled through her with a vengeance. Her heart raced while she leaned against the hard brick wall, wondering what her best move would be.

"Take a deep breath, and calm down," she mumbled under her breath. Never before had she seen such a damned good-looking man.

He was tall and broad shouldered, with a well-worn cowboy hat pulled low over his eyes but the distance between them made it impossible to sense his emotions.

Just her luck. The last thing she could do about it was go flirt with him. "You probably look like hell anyway," she scolded herself. "I doubt he would even notice you."

Within minutes two other men joined the man in the cowboy hat looking at her car. Now what the hell was she supposed to do?

"Breathe." The best thing to do was continue taking small steps to get her car running. It had overheated. She needed antifreeze. If she walked to a parts store, by the time she returned the car would have cooled down.

See. You're organized. Everything is okay.

"We're going to tow your car over to the shop." The deep voice made her jump.

Elsa looked up into deep chocolate eyes, long eyelashes masking his gaze. The man in the cowboy hat now stood way too close, capturing her attention, wearing the look of a predator narrowing in on his prey. Interest and the warm aroma of satisfaction surrounded him. Why would he be satisfied? Her heart stopped beating, the pain building in her chest until she remembered to breathe. He was even better looking up close. Damn.

Sometimes life simply wasn't fair. She would love to have him help her.

"That won't be necessary." Her voice cracked, while her heart began thudding painfully against her ribs.

He moved closer, blocking what sun filtered over to this side of the building. Powerful, well-defined muscles could easily be seen through his t-shirt that stretched across his chest. Thick biceps bulged. The perfect amount of coarse black hair covered his arms. He stood much taller than any man from her pack. As a werewolf he would be enormous.

Like the werewolf you saw last night.

Her pussy swelled, reacting to his male perfection encroaching into her space, her mouth went dry. This was too much man. Too close. Her nipples hardened into painful nubs brushing against the material of her shirt. If she wasn't careful, he would smell her lust.

She moved around him, struggling to regain control. A whiff of salt from his skin, mixed with soap, maybe an aftershave, trailed around her. He captivated her with his all male scent, masculine, rough. There wasn't an ounce of softness to this man.

This werewolf would take over if she didn't assert some authority. An overwhelming urge to tell him her problems, beg him to help her, made her hesitate. But she doubted a weak woman would impress him. She would make him see she wasn't some bitch in need.

She started to walk around him. He moved at the last minute causing her to almost reach out and grab him, just to retain her balance. She wanted to touch him. Muscles

24

moved under his tanned skin when he raised his hand to her face. She held her breath, not sure if she sensed his curiosity, or hers. His fingers grazed her cheek. Electricity charged through her from his touch, gentle yet stemming from so much power. The ache in her pussy returned with a vengeance, heat rushing through her.

He reached for a strand of her hair. "You are too beautiful to be running on your own." His voice had turned gravelly, sending chills racing over her feverish skin.

"That is none of your concern." She moved to walk past him, needing distance before she begged him to touch her some more. He was too much man, too confident in his actions. If she didn't get away from him, she would make a fool of herself.

"You are in my territory. Every inch of you is my concern, moon princess."

What did he just call me?

Her hair was blonde, not white. The only way he would compare her to the moon was if he knew the color of her fur. The thought that this man was the werewolf who had seen her in her fur the night before fueled her excitement. But it shouldn't. She should be terrified. If anyone turned her in, her freedom would be gone forever.

She met his gaze, smoldering heat flushing her skin. She wanted him to be the werewolf from last night. Powerful, larger than life, chasing her, ignoring the fact that she couldn't be caught. She wanted to know if he wanted her as badly as she wanted him. But there was no way to ask him. No way to confirm. Not while he remained a human.

"You are pack leader." She tried to sound indifferent. It didn't matter what his rank was. She had broken none of his laws.

"Tell me where you are staying." His fingers ran through her hair, the urge to turn her cheek into his hand, learn his scent, taste him, overwhelmed her.

He will break your defenses, learn your secrets.

She wasn't born yesterday. Pack leader or not, he didn't need that information. "Not on your life, wolf-man." Drawing in a deep breath, she walked around him, wanting him to see he couldn't make her submit to him.

Even though every cell, every nerve in her body screamed for her to do so.

Thoughts of him pushing her backwards up against the building ransacked her senses. That powerful body could crush her. Imagining his hands gripping her breasts made her nipples pucker with painful cravings. The thought of him rubbing his palm over her tortured flesh, moving her clothes so he could nip at her skin, raised her body temperature to the boiling point.

"Then I will put you somewhere so I *do* know where you are staying." He grabbed her arm, spinning her around to face him.

The two men hovering over her car looked at her with mild curiosity. She glanced at them before the gorgeous pack leader stepped in front of her and blocked her view. His chocolate colored eyes swirled with emotion. Too many feelings to detect all at once. A protector's instinct, strong and raw, dominated over the other array of smells.

His gaze lowered, strolling down her, while something akin to a smile twitched at his mouth.

Wherever he looked, the heat from his gaze burned through her, branding her.

Just fuck me. Put me out of my misery and fuck me, please.

"How sweet of you." Her insides quivered, need consuming her with a fiery craving that burned to her very soul. But she had to sound cool. He couldn't know he affected her. "But I promise you, I'm fine."

"I'll be the judge of that." He didn't seem swayed by her attempt at indifference. "Go inside and eat. I'll get your car taken care of."

This wasn't working the way she wanted.

"I really don't need your help." Her stomach growled, betraying her, and he grinned.

The fire inside Elsa melted her resistance. He could have told her to do anything at that moment and she would have obeyed. Never had a man looked so damned good, his smile simply adding to the perfect package displayed before her.

He moved closer, once again running his fingers through her hair. Only this time he gripped, pulling, forcing her to look up at him. She couldn't move, could only stare into his possessive gaze. Her heart pounded, her pussy throbbed to the same beat, primal, a craving that only he could satisfy. His calm look of authority, pure raw power, of a confidence not faltering, made her shudder.

Thoughts of challenging him, telling him she would eat when she damned well felt like it, entered her frazzled brain. But she couldn't think straight, couldn't form an argument, not with him staring at her like that.

Taking ahold of her arm, he lowered his face to hers, his lips brushing over hers. Heat from his body poured over her, flooding her with his need. That one kiss, the moist heat from his mouth branding her, threw everything she had prepared for her defense to the wind.

More. She wanted more. The kiss ended, a mere touch of the lips. And all she could think of was the emptiness left when he straightened. He brushed her cheek with his thumb, rough and calloused, a working hand. Again, his smile twisted her insides, her pussy throbbing while her heart pounded with excitement. At that moment, she would do anything to learn more about this man.

Chapter Four

Rick didn't want to let her go, didn't want her out of his sight. This sexy little bitch had just landed in his lap. On her own, with car trouble, in his territory. She was now his responsibility. And he took his responsibilities very seriously.

Her blue eyes glowed with a passion and fire that he itched to test. She didn't want to do what he told her to do. She had spunk. Blood rushed through him, the roar of it distracting his ability to concentrate. He remembered the fire that burned in her last night, and her actions today confirmed that passion had not been doused.

She was here, out on her own, her car broken down, telling him she didn't need his help. The adorable bitch was stranded, not that he minded that fact a bit, but she definitely needed his help.

"And how are you going to get the water to your radiator?"

She pursed her lips together, frowning. He was going to enjoy getting to know this frisky female better.

"I'll figure something out." She put her hands on her hips, turning her attention from him to her car.

"Tell Rocky to set you up with breakfast." He turned her toward the diner, wishing he could keep her at his side. "She'll make sure you get a feast."

"I said I didn't..."

"If you stay out here with me, you are going to make me very hungry, moon princess." And he could make one hell of a feast out of her.

Her eyes widened, his meaning obviously quite clear to her. She turned and stalked toward the diner.

"Damn." He watched her tight little ass sway back and forth, his cock growing, pressing even tighter against his jeans.

He needed to fuck her. Wanted more than anything to learn the details of her body.

He looked toward her car, needing the distraction. Damn. She would make the perfect mate. And he didn't know if his heart was ready for that yet.

Joining his mechanic at the car, he realized the man had the repairs under control.

"I'll run and get her some antifreeze." Lyle tapped the lid to the radiator. "She didn't drive it too far. We shouldn't have any trouble getting her ready to go."

Rick nodded, flashing Lyle a knowing grin. "Take all the time you need."

Knowing that the mechanic would have her car in better condition than it had been when it was running, Rick turned and walked towards the diner. Steak and eggs sounded good this morning. Getting to know the story behind his intriguing blonde sounded better.

He strolled across the parking lot, enjoying the warmth of the sun on his back, while thoughts of cornering this female, this alpha bitch, had him grinning. He was going to enjoy this.

Breakfast at the diner had turned into group sessions, something he didn't look forward to. The pack would have congregated by now, everyone having napped after their nightly run, and they would be ready to discuss their problems, pack business and anything else that caught their fancy. Despite his alpha status and his strong responsibilities as leader of his pack, getting to know this alluring woman over coffee and breakfast sounded much better.

Breakfast, with its array of odors, attacked his senses when he pulled open the diner door.

"The usual?" Rocky smiled. She had grown into a beautiful young lady without him noticing. His younger cousin, whom he had practically raised from a cub, seemed to be attracting too many strays lately.

Her soft brown hair, mere shades lighter than his, curled adorably around her face, reminding him of the cub she used to be. But the spread of freckles across her nose and cheeks had faded. And he would have to talk to Harry about getting her a looser fitting uniform. Any tighter and she would be turning heads of every lone werewolf entering the diner.

"I think I'm in the mood for something a bit heartier this morning." He enjoyed her dimples, a small part of her youth still lingering. "Why don't you set me up with some eggs, over easy, and a steak."

She cocked her head at him, her brown curls falling around her face. "Burn a little extra energy last night on your run?"

"That, my dear, is none of your business." He enjoyed watching her blush, and turned quickly to get his coffee and hide his smile.

He wasn't ready for Rocky to turn into a woman of the world, full of knowledge of what consenting adults might do while out on nightly runs.

"I'll have your order up in a few minutes." She placed silverware rolled in a paper napkin down at his usual spot at the counter.

He picked up his coffee cup, blowing on the hot brew, and turned to scan the diner. Usually he would do his best to pick up bits and pieces of what his pack members discussed. None of that mattered this morning.

Rocky leaned forward over the counter. "If you are looking for that woman that came in, she is over there." She gestured with her notepad to one of the corner booths next to the emergency exit.

Rick glanced at Rocky, her brown eyes twinkling with amusement. "Thanks."

He worked his way around the tables, nodding greetings to the morning gatherers, but his attention remained focused on the blonde in the back corner booth. She sat with her back to the wall, glancing down, her hands cupping her coffee mug. She didn't see him approach, but her senses were obviously on alert. She looked up quickly before he made it halfway across the diner.

She glanced at him with haunted looking sapphire eyes. Quickly, the look disappeared, her defenses rising. He could sense her worry, smell the fear and frustration coming from her. An overwhelming desire to wipe all concern from her swept over him, a flushed heat that settled deep inside him. She needed protection. He didn't know why, or from whom. But that didn't matter. She had his protection now.

Whether she would accept it willingly or not was still to be determined. But she would get his protection.

"Have you ordered yet?" He sat down next to her, wanting to be as close to her as possible.

She stiffened immediately, her defenses rising so quickly he swore an invisible wall sprang up around her.

"Coffee is fine." She scooted further from him, pressing tight up against the wall next to the booth.

"I'm Rick Bolton." He held his hand out.

She stared at him for a moment before warily shaking hands. "Elsa Rousseau."

He couldn't let go of her, holding her delicate fingers in his palm. She was warm, although her palm was damp, confirming the nervousness he smelled on her. His heart swelled, an aching sensation he couldn't kick — that this beautiful woman was in trouble and needed him.

"Why are you running?"

She almost jumped at the question, pulling her hand from his. Fear absorbed her nervousness, and for a moment, he thought she might jump over him and run for the door.

"I'm not running from anyone." Her chin stuck out in defiance. She would take him on if necessary. His cock hardened at the thought, her strength appealing to him as much as her beauty.

"Yes. You are." He covered both of her hands with his, and gripped down when she tried to pull away. "And you are not leaving my side until I learn what has you so scared."

Elsa's blue eyes darkened, anger replacing her fear. He loved her array of emotions. So raw and untamed.

"You'll be wonderful company over breakfast," she muttered. "I have no intentions of telling you anything personal about me."

Rocky approached the table, holding a pot of coffee and grinning from ear to ear. "Your order should be up in just a minute, Rick." She placed the pot on the table and glanced at Elsa. "Are you ready to order?"

Rick wanted Rocky to go away. "She'll have what I'm having," he commanded.

"No. I won't." Elsa yanked her hands out from under his. "In fact, I think I've had enough coffee."

Rocky crossed her arms over her chest, still grinning.

Rick wasn't about to let her out of the booth.

"How about just a steak? I can bring it out to you good and raw," Rocky offered.

Elsa nodded, sagging back against the wall.

"I'll have your food out to you in just a minute." Rocky finally left them.

He shifted, turning to see all of Elsa, aching to touch her, but feeling her resistance to him now more than before. She crossed her arms over her chest, an adorable pouty look appearing on her face.

"Look." She turned and braced herself to face him as well, her shirt stretched sideways with her motion, accenting ample, firm breasts. "I understand your concern, being pack leader and all. But really, I am just passing through town. I've already been here longer than I anticipated."

He could see the outline of her bra under her shirt, her puckered nipples pressed firmly against the taut fabrics of her bra and shirt. His cock jerked, the ache in his groin

34

tightening the longer he stared at her. It was her blue eyes, so haunted, yet so beautiful, that compelled him. She was on high alert, not trusting him, and looking ready to flee at the slightest provocation.

"Moon princess. Until I know what has you so terrified, I'm not ready to let you go anywhere." He couldn't keep his hands off of her. Reaching out, he ran a strand of her hair through his fingers. He would die to feel her silky hair caressing his body.

"I'm not scared of a damned thing." She swatted at his hand, her lips narrowing into an angry thin line.

The door to the diner flew open, crashing against the side wall with a loud bang. The strong scent of stale perfume washed across the room quick enough for him to know who had just stumbled in. He didn't have to turn around, or take his gaze from Elsa. He knew without looking that Ramona Rothmeier was about to make an entrance.

Elsa squealed, her hands bracing the table. She appeared ready to jump over it to her freedom in the next second.

Not scared? The woman sitting next to him was terrified.

Chapter Five

Elsa's heart exploded in her chest. She'd just made a complete ass out of herself. What kind of fool had a heart attack because someone walked into the diner?

The waitress walked around the counter carrying two large plates. "Here's your food." She slid one in front of Elsa, and giving the other to the pack leader. "Rick. I think Ramona is drunk again. Can I throw her out?"

"Give her some coffee." A twitch started in a muscle along his jaw. The air around him had lost its relaxed aura. "I'm sure I'll end up ordering her home before long."

Elsa doubted she would be able to eat a bite of the meat in front of her. She glanced toward the door, noticing a young woman dressed in a red mini-dress and heels, obviously she still wore the clothes she had partied in the night before. The woman leaned against the counter, talking to someone, while glancing around the diner. She noticed Elsa and Rick in the corner booth and her lip curled.

Tension swirled around Rick. Elsa picked up on it immediately. Curiosity had her wondering who the bitch at the counter was.

It's none of your business who she is. You need to get out of here.

Unfortunately, that would mean climbing over Rick in order to get out of the booth. Unless she wanted to crawl under or over the table.

The waitress met her gaze, offering a small smile, before turning to carry out Rick's instructions.

"Now then, where were we?" He relaxed almost immediately, once again giving her his complete attention. "You were telling me that you weren't scared of anything."

He grinned at her, that grin that made her melt inside, and added, "Just doors banging open."

His cocky self-assuredness should make her angry. But those chocolate eyes, devouring her while he grinned, left her insides smoldering. He turned to cut his meat, and she caught herself watching the muscles in his arms move. More than anything she wanted to run her fingers over his skin, discover how solid he was, feel the heat of his body.

Her body temperature soared, watching him eat. She was hungry too, but not for the steak. Thoughts of nibbling his skin, tracing paths over those bulging muscles with her tongue, her mind burned with a craving she didn't think herself capable of.

"Eat." He pointed at her plate with his fork.

The steak smelled damned good. The thought of picking it up, tearing into it with her teeth sounded wonderful.

You have been in your fur too damned long.

Within minutes she devoured the entire thing, and put her fork and knife down on the plate.

"Now I should be going." She almost slid into him, letting him know he should let her out.

He didn't budge, his massive presence so close kept her pinned to her spot.

"Where are you going?" He finished his plate as well, then poured them both more coffee.

"Really, Mr. Bolton. That is none of your business."

He straightened, towering over her. In spite of how large he was, she adjusted herself in the seat, refusing to let him intimidate her. Whatever he was looking for, he wouldn't find her lacking. His eyes darkened, penetrating and analyzing.

"Let's go." He surprised her by grabbing her arm, pulling her out of the booth, and heading for the door.

"What are you doing?" She wanted to fight him, tell him he couldn't manhandle her like this.

Curious eyes turned and stared at them though. Every werewolf in that diner gave her and Rick their undivided attention. This was the last damned thing she needed—all this attention.

The way he pulled her along, not hesitating when he opened the diner door, and continued to lead her toward their cars, almost had her panting. She wanted to run into him. Take him on. Forcefully attack him and make him respect her. The thrill of a challenge made the beast within her soar. Adrenaline and lust rushed through her blood.

Rick pulled her between her car and his truck. "Tell me." His piercing eyes burned with desire, darkening his gaze. "Tell me you aren't running from someone."

He pinned her against his truck, his body mere inches from hers. One hand cupped her cheek, his touch burning through her, making it harder than hell to figure out how to answer him.

"Tell me you aren't hiding from anyone. And that when you leave here, you have a specific destination."

Elsa stared into those beautiful eyes that swarmed with emotion. He would hold her pinned here until she answered him. And with his senses heightened by her nearness, he would smell her lie. He had her trapped.

And that pissed her off. "Why don't you go worry about that drunk bitch inside, if you have a desire to run someone's life? Not me. I'm not a member of your pack." She raised her arm to gesture toward the diner, and he grabbed it, pinning her wrist above her head.

"Tell me that you aren't being hunted," he whispered, his mouth hovering over hers.

She couldn't think straight. Even if she fought him, and he would overpower her if she did, that wouldn't help the situation. Already he was too close. His body, all power and domination, was mere inches from hers. It was all she could do not to beg him to press against her, to kiss her, to hold her and protect her.

His free hand cupped her cheek. Then his calloused palm rasped against her skin, moving to her neck.

"Tell me," he whispered again.

Never before had a werewolf tempted her like this. Losing control, giving her care over to another, meant she couldn't handle things on her own. She hadn't run just to stumble over her own paws. No matter how desperately her body screamed for him, her mind knew it was just lust. Granted his words were soft, his determination showing signs of compassion. But she wouldn't give into him

"I can't." Her voice cracked, lust screaming through her while her heart thundered in her chest.

His expression softened immediately. Letting go of her wrist, he took her by the shoulders. "I didn't think so."

He kissed her, his mouth a fiery inferno that burned her alive. She wanted to wrap her legs around his waist, press his cock against her tight, inflamed hole. Her pussy swelled, throbbing, matching the beat of her heart. Without thinking, she pressed her hands to his chest, feeling his heart pound as wildly as hers.

His muscles twitched as she ran her hands across them, giving her power. He wanted her, his lust running as thick as hers. But he would dominate and control her actions if she didn't take a stand. Her freedom was too newfound to allow that.

She broke the kiss, gasping for air when his mouth left hers. Her insides tightened- she wanted him to kiss her again, but had to fight it.

"I can't share anything about me with you, Rick. You need to accept that." She pushed against his chest, ready to walk away from him. Hopefully, her car was ready to go now.

"I won't accept that." He grabbed her, pulling her closer, her tender breasts smashing against his steel hard chest. "And you will not leave my side until I know you are safe."

Chapter Six

Rick turned, his attention focusing on a large work truck that rumbled to a stop in front of Elsa's car. Elsa gave thanks for the interruption. Two men jumped out, and the older, burly mechanic who had looked at her car earlier patted her hood almost affectionately.

"She's full of antifreeze now. You shouldn't have a problem."

"Thank you." Elsa moved around Rick, reaching for her door handle. "I was just getting ready to start it now."

Nodding to Rick, the mechanic climbed into his truck. "Well, I brought Marty over. I'll be at the shop if you need me."

The truck sputtered, heading toward the street, the smell of diesel tarnishing the air. A young werewolf, maybe in his mid twenties, grinned at her.

"How long has it been since I've seen you, man?" Marty flashed a toothy smile at Rick. "I didn't know you had a girlfriend. I'm Marty Rothmeier."

Rick's arm went possessively around her. "This is…" he began, and she cut him off.

She'd be damned if any werewolf would speak for her. "I'm Elsa Rousseau."

What the hell was she thinking? She might as well get on a loudspeaker and yell, "Here I am. Come and get me."

Marty looked at Rick, and then her, giving the two of them a curious glance. "Well, I had Lyle drop me off so

41

that I could walk Rocky home. It was nice to meet you." He nodded to Rick, and gave her a cocky grin, before trotting toward the diner.

Elsa reached for her car door, praying she could get into it before Rick stopped her.

"Where are you going?" He didn't stop her, which almost disappointed her.

"I can't tell you that." She had no idea where she was going.

"Then I'll just have to do some checking around to find out more about you." He crossed his arms across that massive chest, his dark eyes devouring her.

Panic raced through her. If he asked around, put word out to other packs that he'd seen her, asked through the werewolf grapevine if anyone knew her, it would destroy her. Only a matter of time would pass before someone in her pack got wind of his questions. They would contact Rick. And even if he figured out their request to find her was against her will, the damage would be done. Grandmother Rousseau would send her pack members to track her down.

Tears welled in her eyes. She could only blame herself for fucking up like this. If only she had fought Rick, not let him talk to her. Her attraction to him was her own downfall.

She reached for her keys, already in the ignition, but her hand shook so much she gave up, clasping her hands tightly in her lap.

"Please don't do that." Her plea came out with a choked sigh.

Her racing emotions alerted him. She might as well give up running right now. He squatted down next to her, placing his hand over hers.

"Come back to my house with me." His hand rested dangerously close to her crotch, the heat between her legs soaring with the awareness that with the slightest move, he could stroke her pussy. "Tell me why you are running. I will ensure your safety."

Her eyes narrowed. "I don't need you to protect me."

Rick sighed. His patience appeared to be waning. "Don't run like this, Elsa. Let me help you. I can, you know. You want to be free. I can give you that here. You have to stop running eventually."

"I am free." His nearness unnerved her, his hand holding both of hers. The heat from his touch did strange things to her, but she had to keep a clear head. "And I won't give that up."

"You are running. Is that how you want to enjoy this freedom of yours?"

Elsa wavered, wondering if she could trust him. His thumb continued to stroke her clasped hands, almost as if he tried to soothe her. Yet at the same time, desire danced through her from the small motion.

"It won't be like this always." She could feel herself giving in to him.

Those dark eyes swarmed with emotion, something akin to compassion sparked in them, making her want to reach out to him, grab ahold of what he claimed to offer.

"Stay with me. I will assure you pack protection." He raised a hand to her cheek, cupping the side of her face. "Sanctuary, Elsa. Guaranteed. My pack will protect you."

"If I'm found there will be a fight."

"Then we fight, moon princess. But you don't fight alone. My pack won't let you fight alone. Let us help you."

This werewolf—this alpha male—stared at her with a level of compassion, of understanding, that she knew she'd never experienced before. It was as if he knew her pain, sensed her frustration, and offered to shoulder it with her.

"I'll accept your pack protection. So that I can stand and fight. But I won't lose my independence. I won't lose my freedom."

"I will never take your freedom from you, moon princess." His palm caressed her cheek gently, soothing her. "That fire of passion in you is one of the things I find quite appealing."

She wanted to ask what else about her appealed to him. But her stomach already formed a knot from his words.

"Follow me to my house." He stood, and then shut her door, not allowing her the chance to dispute that his pack protection entailed staying at his home.

You are willingly entering his lair. She wondered if she would leave the same woman.

Driving to Rick's house proved more of a challenge than she thought. While following him, she tried different versions of the truth, wondering what the best story would be to tell him. *Try telling him the truth.*

"He won't believe anything I tell him." The truth seemed more preposterous than several of the stories she conjured up.

Telling him Grandmother had assigned three mates to her, George Ricard, Frederick Gambo and Johann Rousseau, and that she needed to give each of them litters in order to strengthen her *lunewulf* breed sounded crazy even to her. Her thoughts strayed to her sisters, Sophie and Gertrude, and her cousin Simone. They had accepted pack law and seemed to enjoy having all those werewolves around. Maybe she was crazy. Most women would probably jump at the chance to fuck three werewolves.

By the time she pulled in behind his truck, her hands shook, her palms were sweaty. She wanted to fuck him and saying no to him while they were alone might prove impossible to do.

Rick hopped out of his truck, approaching her with a confident walk. He looked very pleased with himself, the victor in this round. He had succeeded in pulling her into his domain.

Her legs shook when she got out of her car, staring into the triumphant expression he wore. The way he looked at her, undressing her with his gaze, made her insides boil with need.

"I won't settle for anything other than the truth." He seemed able to read her thoughts, know that she pondered possible versions of the sordid truth.

"There isn't really that much to tell." She stared at his home, a simple ranch style house.

Immediately she noticed the front porch was new. The fresh smell of wood still lingered as she climbed the steps, following him to the door. Pausing a moment, she turned around. What a peaceful view he would have sitting on his porch swing. Fresh cut grass led out to the quiet street, while tall, old trees shaded the area, offering a degree of privacy.

A sense of coming home washed over her, except this wasn't her home. Rick touched her arm, and she turned, smelling curiosity around him while he watched her.

"Do you like it?"

"Yeah. It's nice here." And she liked the pleased look she saw wash over him at her words. What she thought mattered to him.

Unlocking the front door, he stepped to the side, allowing her to enter in front of him. A plain brown couch and two matching chairs were the main furniture in his living room. Everything was clean and in order, but simple. There were no pictures on the walls and plain, utilitarian pillows on the couch. The place lacked a woman's touch.

"There's no reason to be nervous." He came up behind her, gripping her shoulders, then running his hands down her arms.

Electrical currents raced through her from his touch. "I think there are quite a few reasons to be nervous."

Moving away from his grasp, she immediately missed his touch. Feeling cold where the heat from his hands had just been, she wrapped her arms around her waist.

His chuckle, a deep baritone, vibrating through her, confirmed her statement. She had willingly walked into this alpha male's den, placing herself at his mercy, silently giving him permission to do what he would.

"Then maybe the first thing we need to do is focus on getting you to relax."

His phone rang and he gave her an apologetic smile. "My home is your home. I'll be right back."

She watched him leave the room, enjoying the view of his broad shoulders, muscles so solid pressing against his shirt. Her attraction to him puzzled her, making her wonder if she had accepted his pack protection simply because she couldn't fight her pack alone. Maybe she accepted it because she wanted to confront her pack with Rick by her side.

As she turned toward the window, two people walking outside caught her attention, and she watched them, following their path. They headed toward the bungalow next door. After a moment, she recognized the waitress from the diner, Rocky. And the man who had introduced himself to her earlier, Marty, sauntered easily by her side.

She knew Rick reentered the room without turning around. "They make a cute couple."

"He better keep his paws off of her." The protective growl couldn't be missed in his tone.

"He's a bad werewolf?" She looked over her shoulder, noting the firm set of his jaw line, the determined look on his face.

"One of the best werewolves I've ever met." He glanced down at her for only a moment, then returned his attention to the couple outside. "She is just a pup though."

"How old is she?" Rocky looked full-grown to her.

"She is only twenty-one."

Elsa turned to face him. "And how old do you think I am?"

He hesitated, pulling his gaze from the window finally, and giving her his full attention. "How old are you?"

"I'm twenty-three."

He pondered this for a minute, and then his expression hardened. "That is different."

"What is different?" She didn't think she liked what he might be implying. "Am I some woman of the world because I run alone? Does that make me brazen and experienced?"

"Did I say that?" She couldn't read his emotions.

"Well, I'm sure not out on my own because my pack leader thinks I'm too young for a mate."

"Okay." He didn't push her, and she wondered why. "Rocky is my cousin—all the den I have. I'm a bit protective of her."

She nodded. "Just don't try to control her. If Marty is a good werewolf, let her make her own decisions."

"Is that why you are running?" He was reaching into the very depths of her soul. "Is someone trying to control you?"

More than you know, wolf-man.

Chapter Seven

The firm set of Rick's jaw added to the penetrating look that devoured her, stealing her breath. Elsa turned away, running her finger over the top of his television set while staring out a side window toward the small bungalow next door. His presence overwhelmed her, but focusing on something else did nothing to change the fact that he was right behind her.

"My pack has told me whom I will mate with." She didn't know how else to tell him, and prayed her simple answer would suffice.

Suddenly his body pressed against hers, those hard-corded muscles pressing against her backside. Lust swarmed around her. His scent mixed with hers. She loved the smell of domination and compassion mixed so solidly together. The desire to lean back and stretch her body against his distracted her thoughts.

"Isn't that a bit old-fashioned?"

"Yes."

"But there is more."

"It doesn't matter now." She tried to move around him.

"You are going to tell me what I want to know, moon princess." He stopped her, taking her in his arms.

Her hands pressed against his chest, that powerful heat next to her palms feeding her with strength, and terrifying her all at the same time. Fire raced through her straight to her cunt. She looked up at him, his expression intense and dominating. The firmness of his jaw, his lips a determined line, gave her the impression he wouldn't tolerate her hesitation for long. If she told him what he wanted to know, he could destroy her if he couldn't be trusted. But she wanted to trust him. She realized that. The burden she carried weighed her down, running from town to town, living in her fur until a pack discovered her, then moving on. This wasn't how she wanted to live.

"Trust me, Elsa." His mouth lowered to hers.

She responded to his kiss, running her hands up his chest, gripping his shoulders, holding on while she opened to him. Her pussy throbbed with lust that bordered on pain. His tongue met hers in a dance of passion, sending her soaring to a level of desire that she wasn't sure she could handle.

His mouth smoldered. Collapsing against him, she explored with her tongue, allowing him to do the same. Her insides cried to take this further, to learn what this werewolf could offer her.

Trust. He offered trust. Or so he said. Her brain fogged over, his kiss making it hard for her to think. His powerful hands ran down her back, stroking her, gripping her and pulling her closer to him.

"Rick. I…" she breathed against his lips.

"It's okay, moon princess." His mouth left hers, leaving her gasping, while he traced a moist trail to her neck with his tongue.

She didn't think anything was okay. Her pussy throbbed, needing his attention, craving his touch. Her body burned, electricity shot through her everywhere he touched her. Her breasts swelled, aching, pressing against the hardness of his chest. He might request in soothing whispers that she trust him, but his actions demanded her trust.

He gripped her rear end, crushing her against him. The hardness of his cock pressed against her belly, sending her soaring.

"I want you." He growled into the sensitive part of her neck, sending chills through her overheated body.

Lifting her, he moved to the couch. Cradling her on his lap, he buried his face in her breasts, his masculine scent drugging her. He tugged on her shirt, pulling it free from her jeans. The heat of his hand on her belly, and then sliding up until he caressed her breast, sent tremors through her body. She arched into the touch, wanting more, needing him to relieve the swelling ache within her.

He had her shirt pulled over her head before she realized he had the buttons undone. Cuddled in his lap, half-naked, she opened her eyes, focusing on his face, seeing the tormented look he wore.

"So beautiful." His attention went to her breasts, fondling and caressing. Then his mouth rested on a nipple, his tongue swirling it in his mouth. Sensations rippled through her straight to her cunt.

The moist heat swarmed through her, her pussy swelling, cum soaking her. She grabbed his head, pinning him to her breast, needing more of what he was offering.

"Damn. Rick." She cried out while waves of lust rippled through her, her body no longer responding to anything but the need to be satisfied.

Molten lava rushed over her, flushing her with a heat she had never experienced before. His mouth moved to the other breast, nibbling and sucking, while his hand slipped down her body, resting at the top of her jeans.

She should stop him. But her mind no longer controlled her actions. The pressure building inside her needed his touch. She helped him unzip her jeans, lifted her hips so he could slide them down, exposing her pussy so that he could explore.

He lowered her, gently resting her head against the pillows of the couch while he removed her jeans. His fingers ran down her legs, fire racing over her wherever he touched.

"Every bit of you is gorgeous," he whispered. "So beautiful."

His fingers slid between the moist folds of her pussy, testing her, touching the source of her pain.

"Rick. Dear God." She raised her hips, wanting more of him, knowing his touch would appease the incredible pounding that rushed through her.

Spreading her legs, she allowed him space to stroke her, spread her moistness over her entrance. And then he dipped a finger inside her, altering the pressure point within her. She could feel the roughness of his finger stroking the inner walls of her cunt. He satisfied one itch while creating another one all at the same time.

"You are so tight." He sounded surprised.

It took more effort than she realized to open her eyes, watch his hooded expression while he focused on her pussy and the torment his finger applied to her.

"That feels...so good." She couldn't believe what he was doing to her.

Her insides tightened, while his finger probed deeper, moved faster, drawing pleasure and pain together while he fucked her. Her cum soaked his hand, clung to her inner thighs, filled the air around them with a rich, creamy aroma.

"Oh. God." Her eyes drifted shut again while wave after wave of pleasure ripped through her.

She lifted her hips off of him, thrusting herself against his hand, aching for his finger to bury itself deeper inside her. Heat flushed through her, the orgasm tightening every muscle within her, the pressure breaking, a dam releasing fiery moisture.

Collapsing against his hand, his finger still buried deep inside her, she stared at him, his expression wild with predatory satisfaction.

"Rest, baby." He slipped his finger out of her, leaving her satisfied and wanting more all at the same time. "You've just had your first lesson in trust."

Chapter Eight

Rick stood in his bedroom doorway staring at Elsa. He hated to leave her. Never had a woman looked so adorable, given such an aura of defiance, and been so damned innocent.

"Damn." More than anything, he wanted to fuck her.

He watched the rise and fall of her chest while she slept soundly in his bed. Cradling her in his arms on the couch had been the most happiness he'd experienced in a long time. But what he hadn't expected, and still had a hard time believing, was that his moon princess was a virgin.

She'd given no indication. If anything, her wise to the world attitude indicated that she was far from a virgin. But her tough exterior was just that, an exterior shell covering a scared young woman, facing something she had yet to share with him.

"Sleep, moon princess."

The phone rang downstairs. He backed out of his bedroom, enjoying the sight of his sexy blonde lying on his bed. The way she had fallen asleep in his arms, after exploding from his finger fucking, had been a blessing for both of them. Once he'd entered her, experienced how tight she was, felt the limits he could press inside her with his finger, he knew he wouldn't allow her first time to be idle sex.

Grabbing the phone on the third ring, he half paid attention to the conversation, while his thoughts lingered on Elsa. He would have her virginity. He would have her. Regardless of her past, he saw in her a woman willing to fight, capable of taking on the world to get what she believed was right. The traits of a queen.

"No problem, Millie. We'll get that leak patched right up for you." He hung up the phone, and then picked it up again, dialing quickly. "Rocky. I need you to do me a favor. The young lady I had breakfast with is sleeping over here right now. I want you to keep an eye on the place. Let me know if anyone comes or goes from here. Understand?"

"Sure thing, Rick." She said something to someone who was with her.

"Is Marty over there?"

"Yeah. He's here."

"Send him over. He and I have work to do."

Several hours later, after fixing a leak in the roof of the bed and breakfast inn that Millie ran on the other side of town, Marty helped load the tools into his truck.

"So who is the blonde I saw you with?"

Rick couldn't suppress his beast's instincts to claim and protect what he had already decided would be his own. "She's mine," he growled, bristling at the cocky grin his young friend gave him.

"I don't blame you a bit. She's hot. But where did she come from?" Marty walked around to the passenger side of the truck, undaunted by Rick's claim on Elsa.

"I don't know yet." And talking about it made him want to hurry home to continue with his interrogation.

"You don't know. She's running? Are you sure she isn't in trouble?"

"Positive." Rick grabbed the steering wheel, fighting the urge to yank it from the column. "And you'll treat her with respect."

"Of course." One thing he would have to give Marty credit for, the werewolf always knew when to back down. The man wasn't a coward, and made a damned good right hand man, his second in command, but he'd never challenged Rick. Damned good thing, too. Maybe Elsa was right. Maybe Marty wasn't such a bad kid after all.

"Better pull in over here." Marty pointed to the parking lot outside the local pool hall.

One glance at the gravel parking lot surrounding the old building and Rick understood why Marty wanted to stop. He turned into the lot, approaching a couple next to a large motorcycle.

"Well, hell." Rick really didn't care who Ramona Rothmeier spent her time with, but he recognized the werewolf with her. Ramona was part of Marty's den. This wouldn't be good. "That's Ethan Masterson, pack leader out of Duluth. I wonder what he is doing up this way."

Marty didn't answer. But he didn't have to. Rumors were out that Masterson's pack was staking out Rick's territory. Masterson's pack needed hunting grounds. And the werewolf showed all the signs of trying to take over Rick's territory. He was checking out the town, getting a feel for the size of Rick's pack. Rick didn't like the way any of this smelled.

Marty hopped out the second Rick pulled to a stop. "Get in the truck, Ramona. We're taking you home."

Rick didn't see a need to get out but put his truck in park, ignoring the suggestive grin Ramona gave him. "Is the pack leader offering his queen bitch a ride home?"

"This is your queen bitch?" Masterson laughed, leaning forward on his bike, while the hog rumbled underneath him. "I feel for you, Bolton."

Ramona spun around, looking like she would strike Masterson, but staggered and almost fell. Marty grabbed her and pulled her toward the truck.

"We need to talk about all that hunting land north of town, Bolton." Masterson called out to him, while Rick watched Ramona attempt to climb into his truck. She was just about the last person he wanted sitting next to him.

"Nothing much to talk about." Rick knew Masterson wanted rights for his pack to run through the bountiful countryside.

Marty climbed in next to Ramona, and Rick took off, ignoring the grin Masterson gave him. Trouble brewed there, and he didn't like it a bit. Masterson's pack was a lot larger than his.

"Well if this isn't my lucky day." Ramona cuddled next to him, the stale smell of beer and perfume surrounding her turned his stomach. "Drop my little cousin off anywhere, wolf-man, and we'll have some fun."

"What the hell were you doing talking to that pack leader?" Rick didn't mind a bit pushing Ramona into Marty.

Marty looked as repulsed as Rick felt as he grabbed Ramona's wrists and pinned her, so that she couldn't scoot across the seat into Rick again.

"You don't acknowledge my rank. I might as well find someone who does." She turned pouty, her tone assumed a whiny pitch that annoyed him even further.

"You show no respect for your pack. You run with any werewolf who is free that night. How dare you say I don't acknowledge your rank." Rick wanted to wring her neck for disgracing her den in front of a pack outsider. As much as he wished she didn't hold rank of queen bitch, the woman had it by default. "You are the one who doesn't care about the title of queen bitch."

"It's not my fault my sister died in that fire," Ramona spit out. "But like it or not, Rick Bolton, that makes me your queen bitch unless I'm challenged."

"That's enough, Ramona." Marty tugged on her wrists, trying to silence her.

"I know you loved my sister, but she is gone now." Ramona wouldn't stay quiet, and the memories she brought up made him eager to get her the hell out of his truck. "If you gave me half a chance, Rick, I would give you cubs, and make you happy."

"You'd give any werewolf cubs," Rick growled, turning hard onto the street where Marty and Ramona lived while she burst into giggles. "We all lost loved ones in the fire when they burned our pack out of our old homes. But you are going about rebuilding this pack the wrong way."

He hit the brakes hard when they reached Marty's home. Ramona slid forward against the dash. Marty hauled her out of the truck quickly, while she wagged one of her painted fingernails at Rick. "You remember, Rick Bolton. Pack law says I am your queen bitch. Don't go thinking you can replace me now."

He didn't dare tell the woman the thoughts going through his mind, but waited while Marty hauled his cousin across the front yard and into the house. Pack law could be incredibly annoying at times, but dammit to hell, he wouldn't acknowledge a law that didn't better his pack. And that slut didn't care about anyone, let alone herself. She would never be his queen.

Marty looked glum when he walked up to the truck a few minutes later. "You need me for anything else today?"

"No. I'm headed home." He wanted to check on Elsa. Thoughts of her helped remove the disgust he felt over Ramona.

Marty nodded. "I'm heading back inside. I want to make sure she doesn't hurt herself before she passes out."

Rick respected the man for caring for his den mate the way he did. The woman didn't make Marty's life easy, he knew, but the werewolf never complained about her. He would insure Ramona's safety no matter what. The werewolf deserved a den that would make him proud.

Leaving their neighborhood, Rick decided to make a run past the parking lot where he'd seen Masterson to see if the werewolf was still in the neighborhood. While he didn't see him outside the pool hall anymore, Rick doubted the aggressive pack leader had headed back to his own territory. That bothered him, but all he could do for now was put out feelers and see what he could learn about the other pack sniffing around his territory.

Chapter Nine

Sunshine trickled across Elsa's cheek, the warmth adding to the coziness she felt under the blankets. Sleep hadn't been this good in a long time. But what time was it?

Glass panes with simple brown curtains stared back at her as she blinked at the window.

Wait a minute.

The covers pooled around her waist when she sat up, then realizing she was naked, she pulled them up around her. This must be Rick's bedroom. But she was alone. The events of that morning came back to her in a rush, her conversations with Rick, following him over here, and allowing him to finger fuck her in his living room.

Heat flushed over her cheeks and down her neck while she propped pillows behind her shoulders, situating herself in the middle of the large bed. She didn't remember him bringing her to his room.

"I didn't fall asleep while we were..." She couldn't fathom the thought. "I would definitely stay awake for that."

Trying to figure out exactly how she ended up in his bed, she examined the contents of his room. You could learn a lot about a werewolf from his lair. The bed she lay in was sturdy, the intricate decorations hand carved. She turned, running her fingers along the repeating pattern carved into the headboard.

Did you carve this, Rick Bolton?

The phone rang, drawing her from her thoughts. She stared at the phone on the nightstand next to her, its ring following seconds after the ring from a phone downstairs. No one was answering it. Maybe Rick wasn't even here.

The wood floor was cool under her feet when she sat at the edge of the bed. The phone stopped ringing after six rings, the silence of the house surrounding her. She was alone in his home.

An old rocking chair, the padding on the seat worn and well used, sat in the corner of the room. Her clothes had been folded neatly and placed there. She got up and dressed quickly. Curiosity pressed through her, the idea of exploring Rick's home before he returned distracting her.

Now was the time to learn what she could about this werewolf. More than a few things about him intrigued her, and some simple exploring might provide some answers and certainly couldn't hurt anything.

She found two more bedrooms upstairs, both completely empty except for a few boxes shoved into the corners.

"Looks like you do live alone." She liked that thought, although couldn't help wondering why an eligible pack leader wouldn't have a mate.

Trotting down the stairs, she turned into the spacious kitchen. Long cabinets lined the walls above a cluttered counter. A few dishes, mainly coffee cups, were in the sink, and the remains of a steak sat in a take-out foam container on the counter. An open bag of sugar sat next to a coffeemaker, which had been left on. She walked over and flipped the off switch before turning around and glancing through the wide door leading toward the living room.

"I could live like this." She wandered into the living room, the couch where Rick had held her catching her eye.

Moisture still clung to her pussy, while she thought of Rick caressing her, creating a need within her that she'd only dreamed about. The hard cock pressed against her while he played hadn't been her imagination. But he hadn't fucked her.

"You were enjoying yourself, wolf-man." Which is why it made no sense that he'd stopped and let her sleep.

Maybe it's because he won't force himself on you.

She prayed that was the reason. It would be so wonderful if she'd actually found a man who respected her freedom, didn't try to trap her, or control her.

"Or maybe the thought of some young virgin with no experience who is running for her life doesn't appeal to him." She sure as hell had arrived with a load of baggage.

The phone rang again, and she traipsed back into the kitchen, staring at the extension hanging on the wall. After the third ring, she couldn't handle it any longer.

"Hello." She chewed her lip, wondering if she violated any local pack law by answering his phone.

"Oh. Did I dial wrong? I need to talk to Rick." The woman at the other end sounded worried.

"This is Rick's number. But he isn't here right now." She wondered if she should explain who she was.

The woman didn't give her a chance though. "I think my water has broken. Miranda is still out of town buying more herbs. He said he would help me if I needed him."

Rick helped whelp cubs?

"Okay. Calm down. I'm not sure when he will be home. How far apart are the contractions?"

Excited voices came through the receiver from the background. She couldn't be sure, but it sounded like several children talking all at once.

"I'm not sure," the lady finally said. "Maybe five minutes."

Elsa didn't have a clue how to get around in this town. "I know you don't know me." The woman needed to calm down, so she worked to keep herself calm. "But if you give me directions, I will come over and see if I can help."

The woman's shrill cry had Elsa pulling the phone from her ear. "Rocky knows where I live. Bring her, too." The phone went dead in her hand.

She hadn't even found out the woman's name. Elsa stared at the phone. A minute passed before she remembered discussing Rocky with Rick earlier that morning. Rocky lived next door.

Darting out the door, she hurried to the bungalow next door. Someone in Rick's pack needed her and she knew she could help if she could just find out who the woman was and where she lived. She knocked loudly on the door. "You better be home, my dear."

The young waitress who had served her breakfast opened the door, looking half awake. She stared blankly at Elsa, looking her over before concern appeared in her expression. "What's wrong?"

"Hi. Remember me? I'm Elsa. From the diner this morning. You need to help me deliver a cub."

Rocky stared at her a moment before understanding swept across her face.

She knew her concern filled the air around them, because the young woman woke up quickly.

"Shit. Julie went into labor?" She turned into her dark living room, returning a second later with tennis shoes in her hand. "Rick told her to call him. She lost her mate in the fire, leaving her with no den but her cubs."

Elsa led the way to her car, unable to imagine a life without den mates hovering everywhere. She had more cousins than she could count and her sisters had always done everything with her growing up.

That is the life you are seeking out though, isn't it?

The afternoon seemed to disappear as they worked side by side at Julie's house. Twilight surrounded them before the joyful sounds of the newborn cub filled the house.

"You did okay." Elsa patted Rocky on the back, while they both watched mother and cub snuggle under blankets in the small bedroom.

"I've never seen a cub being born before." Rocky sat in a chair next to the bed, her expression glowing, looking proud enough to have birthed the baby herself.

The two of them turned when Julie's older children started talking excitedly to someone who had come to the door.

"Miranda." Rocky walked to the older woman, giving her a hug. "Where were you when we needed you?"

"I just got the message from Julie off of my answering machine." Miranda shoved gray hair behind her ear, smiling at the children surrounding her. "There was another message from Marty. He's looking for you."

"We've been here all day." Elsa glanced out the window, noticing how quickly it was getting dark.

"Oh. Miranda, this is Elsa." Rocky quickly made introductions.

Elsa immediately liked the warm motherly feeling that surrounded Miranda.

"She is the one who dragged me over here when Julie couldn't find Rick."

"Well it's a good thing you were at Rick's to answer his phone. His cell phone never picks up calls. He needs a better service. Miranda shrugged out of her coat, and clasped her herbal bag in front of her. "What brings you to our pack?"

"I'm just visiting right now."

"And she is staying with Rick," Rocky beamed.

Rocky and Miranda grinned, trading knowing looks.

"Well, well." Miranda rocked up on her toes. "Rick Bolton is quite the catch. You would do okay with him."

"Wouldn't there have to be a challenge first?" Rocky asked Miranda.

Miranda gave her a quick, harsh glance, silencing the younger girl. Elsa had no idea how to respond. She wasn't ready to challenge anyone.

"I've...well, I just met him." *Shit.* That didn't sound good.

Obviously Miranda had no desire to allow her to wallow in the humiliating moment. She patted Elsa's arm, and then gave it a squeeze. "It looks to me like you did very well here today. We could use a good bitch in the pack like you."

"We should probably get out of here." Rocky glanced at the wall clock, and then at the window. "It's dark already. I bet Marty and Rick are wondering where the hell we are."

Chapter Ten

"I'm starving." Elsa noticed the grocery store while they drove down the main street of town. "It didn't look like Rick had much food at his house."

Rocky laughed. "He eats what he kills, or at the diner."

"Do you care if we stop?"

Rocky shrugged. "Grab some munchies. Maybe some vegetables. I'll show you this pond up north that is great for fishing. That is, if you plan to run with us later tonight."

Elsa's tummy flip-flopped. She had no idea who Rocky meant by *us*.

Don't get too cozy with this pack. You still have no idea who you can trust, and who you can't.

She didn't want to pay attention to her own words of warning. Rick had offered her pack protection. That meant sanctuary. And she trusted Rick, right?

Damn. She sure wanted to. Her mental vision conjured up an image of him, naked, sprawled out on his bed, beckoning her. Dear Lord. She couldn't wait to explore his body, learn where his scars might be, feel his skin under her fingertips. Hot and hard.

Remembering his cock eagerly pressed against her through his clothes, she wondered what it would feel like to hold him in her hands. She wanted to stroke his steel shaft, watch his expression while she controlled the moment. More than anything, she couldn't wait to return the pleasure to him that he had given her.

"I wonder where Rick is?" she mused out loud, her thoughts still lingering on how she could make that man growl.

"Probably glorifying in how he got out of birthing a cub." Rocky giggled, but then stopped when Elsa swerved to miss a truck that cut her off when she entered the parking lot.

"What the hell!" She focused on her driving, cursing for being distracted by her thoughts.

"That was Toby." Rocky turned, looking behind her at the truck they had barely missed hitting. "I wonder why he did that?"

"Oh. God." Elsa slammed on the brakes when another car pulled out in front of them.

"Are you all drunk?" Rocky jumped out of the car yelling.

Elsa got out on her side. A white sedan had stopped in front of her, and the truck that had almost sideswiped her pulled to a stop at an angle behind her.

"Rocky. Are you okay?" Marty jumped out of the sedan, hurrying toward Rocky.

"Hell yes. I'm okay. But you all were trying to kill us." Rocky glared at Marty, and then at the older man who climbed out of the driver's seat of the sedan. "Harry." She turned her anger on the driver. "What were you trying to do?"

Elsa turned when Toby got out of his truck and approached her from behind. Dark red hair curled around his face while his bright green eyes focused on her and then her car. She smelled concern and worry around him, not alcohol. These men weren't drunk. Something was wrong.

Harry, the older man, pulled a cellular phone from his pocket while he walked toward her.

"Rick. We're at the grocery store parking lot. We found her. Both of them are here."

Tension needled through the air. All the men were high energy, testosterone was heavy in the air around them.

Something must have happened. She could tell they were all pack members, although she only recognized Marty. Rocky obviously knew all of them. But Elsa felt exposed. She hovered next to her car door, wanting to climb back into the car, but curious what the problem was.

"What the hell is going on here?" Rocky asked for her.

Elsa glanced around at the men, anxious to hear the answer.

"Rick's had us on alert all afternoon looking for you two." Harry's words shocked her. She looked from one man to the other, searching for confirmation to what he had just said.

Tires squealed as a second pickup raced into the parking lot. Elsa turned along with the others as Rick pulled up alongside her car and jumped out. He looked so damned sexy in his long straight cut blue jeans and cowboy boots. He wore a denim jacket, the fabric taut across his shoulders, making his chest appear larger. He wasn't smiling, the seriousness of his expression giving him a dangerous look.

In several long strides he approached her, his dark eyes smoldering. She didn't detect the anger on him until he was right next to her. Grabbing her arms, he lifted her up off the ground, pressing her back against the car.

"Why did you run from me, moon princess?" His growl sent shivers through her.

"Run from you?" She stared at him. She'd spent her day helping birth a cub into his pack, and he was bent out of shape because he thought she ran from him? Thoughts of telling him a thing or two faded when she saw the aggravated look on his face.

"What the hell are you talking about?" Rocky cried out.

She turned in time to see Rocky coming around the front of the car. Marty moved to grab her, but Rocky angrily swatted his hands away. She turned to Rick, putting her hands on her hips and glaring at him.

"Elsa and I have been over helping Julie whelp her cub." She glared at Rick. "If Elsa hadn't taken the call at your house, that poor woman would have only had her children to help her give birth."

Rick relaxed his grip on her, and she slid down the side of her car until her feet touched the ground. The tension in the air faded quickly. She turned, staring at the other men who suddenly looked a bit sheepish.

"You were supposed to keep an eye on her for me." Rick's tone softened, but he still sounded put out. "I came home to find both of you missing."

"Keep an eye on me?" Elsa pushed her hands against his chest, needing air. "What? Are you telling me I can't go where I want to go? Am I a prisoner?"

Rick didn't answer her right away, his expression plagued with worry while he looked at her. He ran his rough hand over her hair, brushing it out of her face. His anger had been replaced with concern and worry. She had asked for pack protection, agreed to him keeping her safe. She watched him glance over her head at the small group still gathered around them.

"Thanks for your help, men. Marty, will you drive Elsa's car back to my house? Take Rocky home, too."

"I can drive." She spoke quietly, his gentle stroking making it hard for her to want to do anything but stand here next to him.

"I want you with me," he whispered, just above her ear so no one could hear him but her.

"At least everyone is okay." Toby headed back to his truck.

The others said their goodbyes, while Rick backed away from her car, pulling her along with him so Marty and Rocky could leave.

"You don't know how worried I've been." He turned from her, opening the door to his truck. "Hop in."

The cold of the truck seat seeped through her jeans, feeling good against the tortured heat welling inside her. Rick walked around the front of the truck, his long purposeful strides making him look quite the determined leader.

He climbed in, his truck door slamming shut. Silence lingered around both of them for a moment. Too many emotions cluttered the small cab area. She wouldn't be able to breathe if one of them didn't make an effort to clear the air.

"I offered you pack protection." He spoke before she could sort her thoughts. "But I can't protect you if I don't know where you are. I thought you took off, Elsa."

"Now wait a minute, wolf-man." She had done nothing wrong here. "I woke up to an empty house."

"I have to earn a living." He turned on her, his gaze piercing her.

"I didn't know how to reach you."

"The plan was for you not to go anywhere." The muscles in his arms grew as she watched, the brown curls around his face becoming wilder by the minute.

But she couldn't let him bully her. No way would he put her on a leash, or restrain her freedom. If she couldn't get him to see that, there was no point in pursuing any type of relationship with the man.

"Rick." She took a deep breath, praying for control before she lost her temper. Then she would be running, just to cool off. "Maybe I shouldn't have answered your phone. There were several calls before that one that I didn't answer. But I'm damn glad I did take that call. Julie needed help."

He turned from her, staring out the windshield while he gripped the steering wheel. Without another comment, he put the truck in gear and left the parking lot.

The best thing to do maybe was to cool down a bit. She stared out the window watching businesses go by, and then neighborhoods, while they drove on in silence. He pulled in behind her car, parked in the dark driveway, and cut the engine. She heard him get out of the truck, but kept her attention on her window. He made it around to her door before she could get out of the truck.

Opening it for her, he offered his hand. She searched his face to see what kind of mood he was in.

"Moon princess. Today you acted like a queen. Do you realize that?"

71

She stared at him, his meaning slowly sinking in. Butterflies swarmed in her stomach, her palms suddenly damp. It was one thing to want to fuck him. And she was pretty sure he wanted her, too. But mating? Becoming his queen bitch?

He didn't mean that, did he?

She climbed out, ignoring his hand, then just stood there a moment, her legs suddenly a bit weak.

"I did what anyone would have done today." She wanted to rush past him, hurry inside.

But where would that get her? All she would be doing was leading the way into his den. She crossed her arms, not sure what her next move should be.

"You acted on instinct." He was agreeing with her, accepting the fact that nothing she did today merited placing any kind of label on the action.

He ran his hand down the back of her hair, stroking her, rekindling the fire that had never gone out.

She nodded, unable to look up, afraid of what she might see in his face, not sure she wanted him to know or guess her thoughts.

"Let's go inside."

His words calmed her, making it easy to allow him to guide her to the door. But he had relaxed too easily, and for some reason, she couldn't relax at all. He wrapped his arm around her shoulder, pulling her up next to him while they entered his den.

Chapter Eleven

Relief continued to sweep through Rick while he guided Elsa upstairs. He couldn't remember when he'd last been so upset. All day he'd kicked himself in the ass for leaving her alone in his home. Rocky was no match to control Elsa if she had decided to run. It had made him crazy thinking he'd found the perfect female, and she'd slipped through his fingers before he had a chance to get to know her.

Her silence as he led them to his bedroom showed him she needed time to let his words sink in. But she would accept them. He would allow her time to do so. Elsa was the bitch for him. Never had he been surer about something. He had no intention of ever letting her go.

She met his gaze for the first time when he tugged on her shirt. "What are you doing?" He didn't miss the small fragment of fear in her crystal blue eyes.

"Moon princess, you smell of birth."

"Oh." Her mouth formed such a perfect little circle.

The thought of showering with her made him want to rip her clothes from her body. But gentle might be the better path tonight.

His body clenched, and his cock hardened painfully while he pulled her shirt over her head. Her simple white bra barely contained her full round breasts. Her firm tummy disappeared into her jeans, her belly button barely visible. Reaching behind her, he unclasped the bra, then guided the straps off her shoulders while she watched him.

"Take off your jeans." He knew he would tear them from her, which would more than likely terrify her at this point.

Her blue eyes sparkled, her chest heaving while her breaths came faster.

"You take them off." She challenged him, the hint of a smile forming.

He stared at her for a moment, making sure he'd heard her right. She'd ignored his instruction and countered him. Those blue orbs never strayed, watching him while her nipples hardened, her breathing almost coming in quick, little pants. Maybe she wasn't as terrified as he thought.

Not taking his gaze from hers, he reached between them, grabbing her jeans, yanking the top button free. His coordination was failing him, the zipper not cooperating. He tugged impatiently, refusing to focus on anything but the swirling of emotions on her pretty face.

Finally the zipper loosened, her jeans sliding down her narrow hips. He grabbed ahold of the material shoving it down. Her body swayed into him, but she didn't lose her balance. Never before had such little action on a woman's part made the beast within him stir with such force.

She stepped out of the jeans, standing naked before him. The woman didn't have any panties on. Blood rushed through him, almost blinding him with need.

Turning without a word, she headed toward the bathroom.

"Damn." His own clothes were going to be harder to get off than Elsa's had been.

He fumbled with the buttons on his shirt, finally pulling the damned thing over his head. His boots seemed glued to his feet, not to mention sitting down and bending to pull them off was a pain worse than death. His cock was a rock hard shaft, a steel sword refusing to bend. It would have been easier to simply rip his clothes off.

The water started in the bathroom, bringing thoughts of that adorable ass bending over the tub to test the temperature. Oxygen seemed to be having problems getting to his head. It took some effort to walk to the bathroom, his cock throbbing painfully with every step. But it was worth every moment of discomfort when she turned, halfway into the shower.

"It's about time you got here." She grinned at him and then disappeared behind the shower curtain.

"Woman, I hope you know what you are asking for."

"I wasn't planning on asking for anything." She ducked her head under the water when he joined her.

"What is your plan then, moon princess?" His hands almost wrapped completely around her narrow waist. He pulled her to him, her moist body clinging to his while he wrapped his arms around her.

The grin she gave him made his cock bulge between them. She stretched against him, offering her mouth, which he took eagerly.

He had been wrong thinking she would get skittish on him, or even hesitate. The moist heat from her mouth trickled through him like a drug. Her hands glided up his arms, wrapping around his neck. She leaned into him, relaxing her body against his. She was the most unvirginlike virgin he'd ever met. But how many virgins had he known?

"Baby. Damn." He kissed her damp cheek, moving strands of her long hair behind her back.

The heat from the shower, his throbbing cock, blood pumping too fast through his body, all of it made him question his senses, wonder if maybe he weren't having some wonderful wet dream.

Elsa straightened, stepping back into the water, arching into it so that the droplets sprayed over her face. When she opened her eyes, those baby blues were deep pools of passion, so pure he swore he could see into her soul.

"Elsa." He reached for her, wanting to touch her, needing to have her close to him.

"I want to..." Her innocence had returned, the flush spreading over her cheeks showing him her wanton behavior was due to excitement and not experience.

She went down on her knees before him, looking up at him, her eyes never leaving his. Reaching out, her fingers tracing a delicate pattern over his shaft, she smiled so sweetly, he panicked he would send her flying if he came in her face.

"Be careful, moon princess." He grabbed the base of his cock, the pressure building within making him dizzy.

"I doubt you will break." She put her hand over his, then glided her mouth over the head of his cock.

For a moment, he swore the world turned upside down on him. He braced himself against the shower wall, praying for his vision to clear so he could enjoy the beautiful sight before him.

Water streamed over her while she stretched her lips around his cock. Her tongue darted around his shaft, touching him, licking him, exploring. Her eyelashes fluttered and then closed while she worked more of him into her mouth. It took more strength than he knew he possessed to remain perfectly still and not force his cock deep into the heat of her mouth.

"Elsa." He growled, feeling the craving to grow, his muscles begging to contort.

He fought the urge, knowing the slightest change would alter the size of his cock. He wouldn't allow a damn thing to stop his moon princess from doing what she was doing right now.

"I can't make it all fit." She sounded frustrated.

Her small tongue scoured a heated path down his cock, and he grabbed her hair, holding her head in place. Again the urge to plummet deep inside her mouth, feel her throat contract around him, rushed through him. The beast inside him begged for freedom.

"Trust me. What you are doing is perfect." He groaned. He could barely talk. All of his concentration was needed just to hold still, and allow her to do what she would.

Her tight little mouth wrapped around him again, sucking and licking. She would suck the life right out of him, and he swore that was what she was doing.

"Baby. I'm going to explode."

Her response was to suck harder. She moved her head over him, forcing as much of him into her mouth as she could. Her tongue created havoc, swirling around his cock, stroking up and down.

A dam broke inside him. Pressure released causing a flood of sensation to rush through him. He almost fell forward, but braced himself while his seed sprayed into her mouth. Her lips tightened around his cock head, while she continued to suck.

"Dear God. Elsa!" He couldn't take anymore. Her little mouth, so hot and tight, just about brought him to his knees.

She looked up at him, grinning. "Are you okay?" She didn't look concerned about his wellbeing at all, her smile was too smug.

He wanted to laugh, pull her to her feet, wrap himself around her and never let go. "Yeah. I'm fine."

She stood, her smile not fading, then turned her back to him and adjusted the water. "I assume you joined me to help clean me. Better grab that bar of soap and get started."

Now he did chuckle. He couldn't help himself. His moon princess was feeling pretty good about herself.

"Have you ever done that before?" He reached for the washcloth hanging underneath the soap tray on his shower wall, and began to create a thick lather.

"No."

He loved the view when she leaned back against him, while he ran the soapy cloth over her breasts and tummy. Not one inch of her was ignored. When he knew she couldn't possibly have ever been cleaner, he turned her into the water. Rivers of suds ran down her, circling her breasts, and disappearing between her legs.

She didn't try to talk, which was fine. Nothing distracted him from stroking every inch of her. The heat from her pussy reached his fingers before he pressed through her smooth folds. Thick cream clung to his fingers and he enjoyed watching her eyelashes flutter over her darkening blue orbs. Her breathing increased when he eased his finger inside her, humidity flushing over his hand.

"Will you fuck me this time?" Her question startled him, her expression not changing when she asked.

She looked sated, lazy, steam from the shower billowed around her.

"Do you want me to?"

"Yes."

His cock danced to life with that one little word. Sliding his finger out of her, he reached around and turned off the water. She pulled the shower curtain back before he could, her eagerness undoing him. Reaching for the towels, she handed him one, then stepped out and ran the other one over her body. Every curve, every tight, firm spot on her body glowed from the heat of the shower and the invigorating rub she gave herself with the towel.

He barely ran his towel over himself, not caring if water droplets ran down him. The enchanted beauty in front of him toweled her hair, then combed through it with her fingers. He couldn't look away from her.

Nothing remained of the skittish female he'd brought home. She stared at the fogged over mirror, appearing to appraise herself as she finished wringing out her hair with her hands. He enjoyed the view, her full breasts perky with nipples hardened into sweet brown peaks. The sweet curve of her ass, and thin, muscular legs made her a picture of perfection.

His perfection. And he was about to place his mark on her permanently.

"You're dry enough." He stepped out of the shower, tossing his towel on the toilet seat.

"You wouldn't believe how wet I am." She didn't blush when she met his gaze, although the heat in her eyes made his temperature soar.

Turning her toward the bedroom, he walked behind her while she allowed him to guide her to his bed. Pressure soared to a dangerous level inside him when she crawled on all fours in front of him onto the mattress.

"Are you sure about this?" He didn't want to ask her. Didn't want to give her the opportunity to change her mind. But even if she didn't act like it, he knew from his explorations that another werewolf had never fucked her.

And another werewolf would *never* touch her.

"If you don't want to do this, just say so." She rolled over, her look so coy and tempting that he growled in spite of himself.

"Woman, I've wanted inside you since I first laid eyes on you." He crawled over to her, eager to taste her.

She cried out when he sucked her puckered nipple into his mouth. The hardened flesh tasted clean, and so sweet.

"Rick." She grabbed his hair, pressing his face against her breast. "God. Don't stop."

He had no intention of stopping. She arched off of the bed, her orgasm filling the room with its rich aroma. He couldn't believe how sensual her body had become. Ripe and willing, offering him cream never tasted before. He had died and gone to heaven.

"Everything about you." He started a path of kisses down toward her belly button. "Perfect. So perfect."

She giggled, pressing her hands against his shoulders while she spread her legs. "I'm not perfect, wolf-man."

Like hell she wasn't. He wouldn't argue with her though. Her pussy opened up for him, her legs stretched, allowing him to slide down between them. Soft folds glistened with her juices, her tiny hole glimmering with clear moisture. He traced a finger over her cunt, her body jerking from the small motion. He watched her mouth open with a silent cry, a vision of beauty so raw and untamed he couldn't believe it.

"Oh. Shit." She bucked against him when he ran his tongue down the length of her pussy.

Heat swam around his face, matching the intense fire building inside him. His cock throbbed against the bedspread underneath him, demanding attention. Pressing his lips to her clit, he sucked and licked, holding her in place while he feasted to keep her from bouncing off the bed.

"Dammit. Rick." She cried out, her muscles tightening enough that he knew the change threatened her.

"What do you want, moon princess?" He enjoyed her tormented expression.

"You know."

"Tell me."

"Fuck me. Please fuck me." She opened her eyes, her gaze imploring him.

When he climbed over her, she watched his cock. Her moist heat soaked his cock head, making his blood boil. The overwhelming urge to dive into her almost consumed him. He couldn't move for a minute, working desperately to control the beast that threatened to emerge, take over and claim his queen.

Elsa must have sensed his battle, because she stilled. When he thought he could move without endangering her with a roughness she wasn't ready for, he met her gaze, seeing wonder filling her eyes.

Her hands slid down his chest, but he grabbed them. "I will control this." If his order confused her, she didn't complain.

"Then take me," she whispered.

Fire soared around his cock as he pressed inside her, entering her narrow hole. For a moment, he thought her heat would suffocate him. So tight. So wet. Nothing had ever felt this damned good before.

He buried his cock deep inside her, until she had stretched enough to take all of him.

"Breathe, baby." He watched her gasp, knowing his size overwhelmed her.

She didn't cry out though, made no indication that he hurt her, but continued panting, while she attempted to smile.

"It's good." Her eyes glowed like deep pools of sapphire. "So damned good."

He could hold still no longer. Pulling out, he lost himself in her again, moist heat flaring around him, driving him further inside her. With each plunge he watched her body jerk, her eyes widen, while she dug her nails into his shoulder.

He growled, closing his eyes while he exploded like he hadn't come in months. "You...are...mine!"

Chapter Twelve

The mixed odors of fish frying and coffee brewing made her stomach growl when she walked into the diner late the next morning.

Rocky leaned against the counter talking to a lady Elsa didn't know. She hesitated in joining them. Coming here at all gave her the jitters. Maybe she should just drive over to the grocery store, buy food, and then not have to worry about leaving Rick's house at all. Every time she went out in public, she risked someone recognizing her and sending word to her pack.

And how long are you going to hide out at his place?

"Elsa. Come here." Rocky waved to her, gesturing for her to join them.

So much for turning tail and running. Her heart raced a little faster when she walked past several werewolves who gave her curious glances.

The young woman sitting by Rocky gave Elsa the once over. Maybe it was her imagination but recognition seemed to wash over her expression. Fear gripped her gut, twisting it into a knot.

"Elsa, this is my friend, Samantha." Rocky grinned while gesturing from one lady to the other.

"Hey." Samantha brushed pale blonde strands of hair away from her pale brown eyes. "I've heard a lot about you."

"You have?" If the pack was talking about her, things could be worse than she realized. She needed a cup of coffee. The urge to get the hell out of the diner grew inside her. But showing panic would raise even more questions. She took a slow calming breath. "All good, I hope."

The woman's complexion was fair enough to be *lunewulf*. She guessed the woman dyed her hair since it was almost white. A dab of color on her eyelids, with dark eyeliner and dark lipstick added an air of mystery to her.

"Rocky told me all about how Rick sent the pack on full alert looking for you two yesterday." Samantha's smile relaxed her features a bit although it still seemed she eyed her carefully.

"He didn't put the pack on full alert because of me." Rocky laughed, while walking around the counter to grab a pot of coffee. She poured the hot brew into cups for all of them. "My cousin was in pure alpha form looking for this chick here."

Samantha's gaze filled with laughter while she watched Elsa over her coffee cup. The best thing to do was appear amused by the situation too. But this kind of idle chatter could be the end of her. Anyone could overhear them. Even if these two were trustworthy, their easy sense of gab could steal her freedom, if not her life.

"Well, I just stopped in to say hi." Her stomach growled, proclaiming her a liar, but she ignored the hunger pangs. "I have some errands to run."

The door to the diner opened behind her, a cool breeze surrounded her, giving her a chill. Winter would be here within a few short months. If she weren't careful, she would enjoy the cold nights in her fur, hiding in a cave.

Maybe she could head further south, get lost somewhere in the States. Thoughts of Rick made that a very unappealing idea. His strong warm body wrapped around hers protectively, his soft breathing while he slept, she didn't want to give that up.

Not to mention the way he'd fucked her. More than anything, she wanted to be with him again, explore the different sensations he'd introduced to her the night before. Her body warmed just thinking about how he felt buried deep inside her. His dark eyes, smoldering while he watched her come. His large calloused hands touching her everywhere. The way he had brought her body to life, made her crave more of every sensation he'd given her. Rick made her feel more cherished than she'd ever felt before.

"Look who the cat dragged in." Rocky grinned from ear to ear.

Elsa glanced toward the door, immediately noticing Marty. He scowled at Rocky, but pulled her into a bear hug the second he reached her. The cozy warmth filling the air around the two of them made it hard not to smile. This was unconditional love. She was sure of it. Happiness found simply in being with each other.

"Hello, Ramona." Samantha's tone caught Elsa's attention. A cold emotion not easily identified surrounded the blonde woman.

She turned to see the woman who had been drunk in the diner the previous day.

"Who do we have here?" Ramona blew on long pink fingernails, then flashed her cold brown stare at Elsa. "Oh. You're that blonde who likes pack leader cock."

Hairs raised on the back of her neck, her blood thickening with the urge to allow her fingernails to grow just enough to leave marks when she slapped that cold glare off Ramona's face.

"Ramona." Marty gave her a warning look, changing the warmth surrounding him to something more sinister.

"And you must be the pack alcoholic." Elsa knew she should hold her tongue, not draw unwanted attention to herself, but this woman needed an attitude adjustment.

Samantha snickered. Rocky looked surprised. But Elsa held her ground, staring at the woman who glared with an icy blue gaze that turned mean.

"Watch who you are talking to, little one." Ramona pointed her pink fingernail at Elsa. "You are talking to the queen bitch. I'll kick your ass right out of this town."

She didn't hear her right. Elsa's heart pounded painfully in her chest, the diner suddenly seeming to close in around her.

"What did you say?" She could hardly speak.

Ramona laughed, more like a cackle. "Oh. Did Rick fail to mention that small detail to you?"

"Elsa. It's not…" Rocky silenced when Ramona held her hand up.

Anger and humiliation flushed over her, burning her skin. This couldn't be happening. Fucking Rick last night still had her tingling. The afterglow had warmed her body all morning. Thoughts of cleaning his house, spending some of her money on food, and preparing a nice meal for when he came home later had entered her mind.

He said, "*You are mine.*" How could he have said that if he was already mated?

"Don't get your claws buried into Rick Bolton, little bitch." Ramona took a step toward her, smacking Marty in the chest when he tried to pull her back. "You can't have him."

Rocky wouldn't look at her but instead focused on Marty, worry streaming across her pretty face. Samantha, on the other hand, looked pissed, her lips pursed while she stared at the ground. Marty didn't look too pleased either.

The array of emotions spreading through her made it hard to think. She stared at Ramona, wanting to demand how she could be mated to Rick when it appeared she didn't live with him. Frustration at the thought that she would reveal knowing what his bedroom looked like had her fumbling for the right words.

But then a wash of clarity brought reality back to her. This wasn't her pack. Rick wasn't her pack leader. She didn't want these werewolves to know anything about her. Nothing good could come from challenging Ramona at any level.

Her heart weighed heavy while she struggled to remain calm. Without saying a word to any of them, she turned and walked out of the diner, hoping she at least held on to a shred of dignity.

Ramona's laughter, which hit her before the diner door closed behind her, made her blood curdle. More than anything, she wanted to turn and attack, slapping that painted face hard enough to make her feel better.

You can't draw attention to yourself.

Sure looked like she'd failed there. A handful of the werewolves in this pack watched her leave the diner. She had screwed this one up pretty bad.

Some sense of self-esteem returned as she managed to drive back to Rick's house without shedding a tear. That must have helped clear her head a bit. It dawned on her that Rick had offered her pack protection. Nothing more. Last night she had asked him to fuck her.

"He is an alpha male, dammit." She cursed her own naïvety. Nothing more than her own gullibility was at play here. "You asked him to fuck you."

More than likely, all alphas laid some kind of claim on any woman they fucked. Added them to their territory. It didn't sound like a very nice thing to do, and sure didn't make her feel a damn bit better. But it made sense if he had a queen bitch. Maybe he laid claim to making her a piece of tail on the side. A small payment for giving her pack protection, seeing to her safety.

Now that you've made him out to look like a complete jerk, do you feel better?

Gloom trickled through her while she parked her car in his driveway. Making Rick out to be an ass did nothing to cheer her up.

The phone rang the second she let herself into Rick's house. Walking into the kitchen, she stared at it. This wasn't her home, whoever called was none of her business.

But yesterday answering that phone had helped someone in need. Rick was pack leader, and whether he had a queen bitch working with him to lead the pack, or not, dens of werewolves relied on him. That phone call could be important.

She grabbed the phone. "Hello."

"Elsa. Thank God you went back to Rick's house." It took her a second to recognize Rocky's voice on the phone.

She laughed, her forced attempt at joviality adding to the sinking feeling growing inside her. "Where else would I go?"

"This is Rocky. I had to wait for Ramona to leave before I could call you." The clattering in the background had Elsa envisioning Rocky standing in the kitchen, using an office phone. "You really should come back down here. There is something you should know."

"What's that?"

There was a pause, the sounds of the kitchen filtering through. Looking around the quiet house, she imagined taking on this bachelor's kitchen, cleaning and cooking.

This isn't your home.

"It would be better to tell you in person. Come back down here, please. I'll have breakfast and coffee ready for you."

Chapter Thirteen

Rick had visions of wringing that little slut's neck while he listened to Marty relay the confrontation that had occurred at the diner earlier that day. Grabbing his cell phone from his belt, he punched in the numbers to his house.

"No one is answering." And he was stuck at the Mulligan's house until he finished fixing the loose stairs on their front porch. "Ramona better not send Elsa running."

"We could put a man or two on her. Keep an eye on her," Marty suggested.

Even though Ramona was Marty's den, he knew the werewolf got tired of her antics. The bitch pushed the limits on her title by default too often.

"Call Toby. I can't get away from here for at least another hour." If his sexy blonde ran from him, he would spank her adorable behind. "Tell him to keep a tail on Elsa, but not to let her know he's watching her."

Marty nodded, turning to head back to the car he'd borrowed from Harry to come talk to him. Obviously, Ramona's little outburst at the diner had sent half the pack into a frenzy. He appreciated Marty coming and telling him though.

"Ramona threatened the women if they talked to Elsa."

Rick almost hit his hand with his hammer. He sighed. Dropping the hammer to the ground, he stood, facing the werewolf.

"Elsa doesn't need to know that. I still don't know all the details, but she is running from her pack. I won't have my pack hurting her."

"Running from her pack?" Marty stared at him, apparently wanting to hear more.

"I don't want her running from this pack." And she wouldn't run from him.

"I told Rocky to call her as soon as Ramona left. The women won't ignore her."

Rick watched Marty leave before turning back to the steps. Images of her baby blue eyes, so full of life, eager to learn and explore new things, popped into his head. Whoever had hurt her in her past would suffer, he'd already decided. Now he had Ramona to deal with— again. That female was a thorn in his side.

Of course, Elsa had the right to challenge her. If she decided she wanted her title, truly wanted to be his mate, she could call Ramona out. The only way Elsa could be queen bitch would be to kill Ramona. And that would be a fight he would love to see.

Imagining that trim body, so soft yet so firm, he began pulling nails from the rotted wood on the staircase. He'd explored every bit of her last night while showering and then fucking her. Nothing had ever brought him more satisfaction than hearing her cry out his name while she came. The way her nipples had hardened into perfectly round pebbles. Watching her taut belly rise and fall with her gasps. Feeling her long blonde hair glide over his fingers as it fanned around her while she'd tossed her head from side to side. Her body had cried for more of him, absorbed his cock into her heat and clung to him tighter with every orgasm.

Elsa had watched him with those sensual blue eyes, and briefly, during the intense heat of their passion, he'd watched her ghosts leave her. True happiness and contentment had washed through her.

He imagined right now her past riddled through her, while the incident that had just occurred at the diner added pain to her misery.

It would not continue. He would not allow her spunky spirit to be beaten until broken. The woman had entered his life for a reason. That point would not be argued. And he would be damned if she would suffer any longer now that he had her.

Finishing the stairs didn't take too long. Calling his house again, he growled when the phone rang through to his voice mail. *Where the hell was his sexy, blonde werewolf?*

After loading his tools back into the van, he decided to check in at the diner, see if Toby had tracked her down. The werewolf better have found her.

"What the fucking hell?" He parked his truck in front of the diner, and stared at Elsa's car, parked across from his.

All four tires were flat. A man he didn't recognize stood next to the car, inspecting the tires. He walked from back to front of the car, then squatted, running his finger along the wheel.

Rick had seen enough. This werewolf walked around Elsa's car like he owned it.

Getting out of his truck, he enjoyed watching the man straighten quickly when he slammed his truck door closed. "What are you doing?"

A calm, almost cocky expression remained on the werewolf's face, even though his body tightened. Rick knew the kind. An alpha male had entered his territory. He didn't recognize this werewolf though, and he hadn't approached through the usual channels if he were a pack leader searching out new territory.

"I wish to speak with your pack leader." A wave of annoyance leaked through the man's demand.

"You're talking to him." Rick maintained eye contact, willing the man to show his respect, acknowledge his rank and wipe that cocky look off his face.

The man grinned, none of his calm self-assuredness leaving. He extended his hand in greeting. "I'm Johann Rousseau."

Rousseau. Elsa's last name was Rousseau. Ignoring the greeting, he walked around the werewolf, aware of how alert the man stood, his calm friendly approach not hiding the underlying tension slowly filling the air.

He wouldn't hide his feelings, not wanting to mask the fact that he would fight and protect what was his. And Elsa belonged to him.

"What are you doing here?" If the werewolf had just slit Elsa's tires, he smelled no guilt on him.

But one glance told him her tires had been slashed. Without looking too closely, he would guess a werewolf had extended its claws swiping each one. Anger raced through him so quickly, he considered pounding the intruding werewolf first and questioning him later.

"I heard Elsa was here." Johann Rousseau nodded to Elsa's car. "You know where she is?"

He would be damned if he admitted he had no idea where she was. "Why do you want to find her?"

The werewolf met his gaze. His blue eyes were so similar in color to Elsa's. His pale blond hair, cut short, didn't have that silky shine to it though. And he sure didn't have her good looks.

"I'd like to know that she is okay. That she is happy." Something changed in the werewolf's expression. Rick smelled it while he watched the man's gaze harden. "Where is she?"

He would not be challenged. No alpha male sauntered into his territory making blind demands. "Where are you staying? If she wants to contact you, she will."

The werewolf shrugged. "I just got here. Haven't found a place yet."

Rick noticed the Canadian tags on the blue Suburban parked a few stalls down. It would be easy to spot. He had no interest in offering the werewolf housing, but knowing where he was might be a good idea. But first things first.

He didn't doubt the werewolf would follow him when he headed toward the diner. Johann Rousseau was on his tail when he entered, taking in the few loiterers. Harry headed toward him from the other side of the counter the second he saw him.

"Get the man some coffee." He waited until Johann sat at the bar, nursing a cup and then gestured to Harry to join him at the other end. "What the hell happened to Elsa's car?"

The older man ran his hand through his thinning gray hair. "You missed some action."

Chapter Fourteen

Elsa slowed to a walk, the sting on her cheek reminding her how badly she'd humiliated herself. The best thing would have been to stay out of the whole damned thing. But she hadn't and now the damage was done.

"Hey. Wait up." Rocky trotted down the sidewalk behind her. "I can't believe your car."

Her car was the last thing she wanted to think about right now. Sitting in the middle of the diner parking lot, right along the road for anyone to see, and stuck there with flat tires. She'd made a spectacle of herself, and left her damaged car as a reminder.

Shit.

"I'm sure Ramona did that to your tires." Rocky caught up with her, holding her work apron in her hand while she matched Elsa's pace.

"After the way I stood up to her in front of her pack." She could kick herself a million times for not thinking. "I wouldn't be surprised."

More than likely by now, the entire pack knew how she had told Ramona off. She ran her fingers over her cheek, certain it had puffed up like a balloon by now from Ramona slapping her.

"You were great." Rocky nudged her, grinning from ear to ear, like they were best of friends. "She teases me all the time. You stood up for me."

"She shouldn't ride your ass about being a virgin. And the comments she made to you about Marty…" Just thinking about how Ramona had told Rocky she was a prick-tease around Marty made her bones pop. Adrenaline rushed through her while the urge to change made her body ache.

"Marty and I can't mate," Rocky mumbled so quietly that Elsa almost didn't hear her. "Ramona says he can't take me as a mate. And since she is the elder in his den…and queen bitch…"

"You two would make a perfect mating." Elsa knew her anger would surge out of control all over again if she didn't drop this. But none of it made any sense to her. "Why does she say that?"

"I'm sure it's because Rick won't take her as a mate."

Elsa stopped in her tracks, positive she didn't hear right. "She is queen bitch. Doesn't that mean she is Rick's mate?"

Rocky shook her head. "Rick had a mate. Ramona's older sister. She's dead. When we were all still in Duluth, our pack was burned out. We lost almost everyone. Rick relocated us here. You know, small town, low profile. Anyway, Ramona became queen bitch by default. There is no one to challenge her."

Rick didn't have a mate. And last night he said, "You are mine."

She realized they were walking again, Rocky strolling alongside her, watching her curiously. They reached the quiet lane where Rocky and Rick lived. Elsa studied Rick's house while they walked toward it.

If you challenge Ramona, you could have Rick.

"What are you thinking?" The silence must have grown too thick for Rocky.

"I need to figure out what to do about my car." That hadn't been what she was thinking at all. But she wouldn't share her ridiculous ponderings with Rocky.

Her pack was looking for her. And she already had three mates. Just a minor problem that she had no idea how to take care of.

"I doubt you have to worry about your car." Rocky walked ahead of her, heading for her small cottage next to Rick's house. "As soon as Rick sees it, he will make sure it's taken care of."

She turned around, grinning conspiratorially, but then frowned, looking past Elsa. "There's Toby. I hope nothing's wrong."

Turning, she made eye contact with the redhead driving toward them in his truck. He leaned over, rolling down the passenger window. "I'm supposed to tell you to get in touch with Rick."

Elsa's heart pounded in her throat, her palms suddenly growing damp. Rick must know what happened. Now she had to figure out how to justify her actions to him.

Her cheek must have been a sight the way Toby focused on it.

His boyish grin made her warm with embarrassment. "Looks like I missed a show."

"You sure did." Rocky sounded ready to share exciting news. "Elsa could have kicked Ramona's ass if she wanted to."

"Do you want to?" Toby grinned.

This pack needed a good queen bitch so desperately. *And you need a good pack.*

The lump in her throat prevented her from answering.

"Don't push her." Rocky put her arm around her. "Give her time to get to know Rick."

This pack was sucking her in. She could feel it. "I guess I should call him."

"I think that would be a good idea." Toby revved the engine on his truck. "Be good, you two."

Her thoughts drifted to Rick while Toby turned his truck around and headed out. She wondered if he had noticed her car. More than likely if he had, he'd already heard about the little scene she'd had with Ramona in the diner.

Dammit. The entire pack is probably buzzing over the latest gossip.

"I think I'm going to take a nap. Do you want to run later?"

Elsa knew running with any of the pack would only make them talk more. She looked different as a werewolf, her glossy white coat and smaller size, strong traits of her *lunewulf* breeding. At the rate she was going, she might as well contact her pack. There wouldn't be a werewolf in the entire territory that didn't know she was here. So much for keeping a low profile.

"Maybe. I should take a nap too."

Rocky grinned, then turned toward her cottage. Elsa stared at Rick's house for a moment. Its strong silence seemed to reach out, offering her sanctuary, protection.

Curious to see what her face looked like, she trotted up the stairs to the bathroom. Faded green swelling spread over her cheeks. Several scratches from Ramona's extended claws trailed down the center of the bruising. As she ran her fingers over the bruise, images of Ramona's furious glare told her how cold-hearted the bitch actually was. The woman didn't care at all about Rocky or Marty's happiness. And it was clear as the nose on her face that the two of them were in love.

"You don't deserve to be queen bitch." She stared at her reflection, reaching for her brush and running it through her windblown hair.

But Rick should have told her about Ramona. He'd intentionally kept that information from her. *But you haven't told him you are running from a pack that wants you to mate with three werewolves.*

Sighing, she turned away from the bruised face in the mirror. Now she had to figure out what to say to Rick.

The front door downstairs opened and closed just as she reached the phone next to the bed.

Shit.

Loud footsteps bounded up the stairs. Rick appeared in the doorway, looking larger than life. Adrenaline pumped through the air around him. His brown hair, windblown around his face, made him appear almost wild. His chocolate eyes swirled with emotion, pinning her with a dark, haunted gaze.

"Will you challenge the queen bitch, moon princess?" He moved across the room, towering over her.

"You should have told me there *was* a queen bitch."

His immense size could be intimidating. So much werewolf. So much man. His sensual aroma, mixed with passion and anger, made her heart race. Her fingers itched to touch those powerful chest muscles.

"Would that knowledge have changed anything?" His calloused fingers snaked through her hair, easing her head back so that she stared into his questioning gaze.

"You can't claim me if you already have a queen bitch."

"I already have claimed you." His mouth lowered to hers, hot, burning, branding her while his words swarmed through her brain.

He pressed her to him, his other hand sliding under her shirt, searing her back with his touch. She cried out into his mouth, unable to help herself. His actions were almost wild as he yanked at her shirt, making her stumble backward as he pulled it over her head.

"You can't claim…"

Her words were lost when he captured her mouth again. A bruising kiss, filled with fire, a domination that would crush any obstacle to gain what he wanted. What she needed. Yes. She needed this.

His aggression filled her, wrapping around her like a gusty wind. His mouth seared her swollen cheek, traced a burning wet trail to her neck, showing her he didn't care about pack law.

Towering over her, filling her senses, her vision, everything around her with his presence, he ripped at her jeans as she tripped backward. She was certain buttons flew. His wild behavior brought on a portion of the change in him, his fingers thicker, nails a bit sharper while he yanked her jeans down her legs.

The coolness of the wall against her back did little to soothe the heat racing through her. Words no longer seemed important. This beast/man ravished her, his large hands gripping her breasts, squeezing and pulling while his mouth seared over her with a heat that filled her with need. A lust-filled fever flushed through her, tormenting her with an ache that craved more of him.

"Rick. Shit."

His tongue lapped at her nipple, moist fire searing from the focus of his torture, straight to her pussy. Grabbing his shoulders, feeling the taut skin covering his solid muscles, she wanted to pull him inside her, force him to soothe the fever he'd created inside her.

"Every inch of you," he burned a path with his tongue down her abdomen. "Is mine."

Expert hands glided down her body, while he tasted her flesh, licking, nibbling, wave after wave of passion rippling through her like an angry gale wind. Her feverish senses riding a tide that built with fury, anticipating the pending storm.

His fingers pressed against her flesh, gripping her hips while he knelt in front of her, his breath hot against her skin.

"Come on my face, moon princess." His tongue pressed through her sensitive folds, stabbing her swollen pussy.

"Rick. Oh. God." Her head fell back, hitting the wall behind her, its solid coolness doing little to hold her up against his attack on her cunt.

His tongue lapped at her moisture, drinking her cum while she held on to him. His solid muscle her lifeline while he fucked her with his tongue.

The world would collapse around her. She was sure of it. The roughness of his tongue stroked her clit while he gripped her hips, holding her in place, pinning her while he devoured her. The tightening of her womb, a quickening building within her, made her dizzy, craving to give him all that he wanted.

A low growl, vibrating from within him, seared through her overheated senses. This was only his tongue. His ability to know just how to touch her, stroke her, bring her body to a point she never knew she could reach, overwhelmed her. Nothing she'd ever imagined, ever dreamed of while playing with herself, matched what he did to her right now.

"Rick. Help me." She would go over the edge. Her world seemed to tumble to the side. Even with the wall behind her, and him holding on to her, she couldn't stand.

Wave after wave of heated passion gushed through her, her body crashing against a storm that riveted through her with enough force to steal her breath. Grabbing his head, gripping his coarse hair with her fingers, she rode the storm that rushed through her, fearing she would pass out from the intensity of it.

His tongue lapped the cum that soaked her pussy, while she struggled to breathe. Her legs suddenly wouldn't hold her, the intensity of her orgasm taking all of her strength.

Powerful arms grabbed her when she collapsed over him.

"You are already claimed," he whispered, lifting her and carrying her to the bed.

Chapter Fifteen

Rick stared through the window, squinting at the sunset. Propping the phone against his shoulder, he searched for coffee filters. He had a feeling it would be a long night.

"I'm an understanding man." Ethan Masterson broke up slightly on his cell phone. Rick wished the connection would break up altogether. "But my pack is ten times larger than yours. We need good hunting ground. I think I'm being more than fair allowing you time to round your pack up before settling in."

He wanted to tell Masterson to kiss his ass. The werewolf in him itched to come through and run the punk out of town. And Rick would love to take the man on, humble him down a few notches. But the sad matter of fact was simply that his pack had endured enough over the past few years. He didn't have the wolf power to stop Masterson's pack from taking over.

"I'll bring it up at our next pack meeting." And he was being more than fair by not telling the werewolf no. Even if it was a fool's mission.

"I'll give you a week." Masterson hung up the phone.

He squeezed the receiver, aching to hurl it against the wall. A week. Where would he take his pack? Funds were low. Everyone had just settled in to jobs after relocating from Duluth. Life had just started to feel normal again.

Deciding against coffee, he turned toward the stairs. His moon princess had been asleep for several hours now. Thoughts of cuddling that silky warm body against his sounded a hell of a lot better than plotting how he was going to get his pack out of town.

Just staring at her helped ease the throbbing headache that had started at his temples. Elsa lay cuddled into a ball, the blankets tucked around her. One hand rested next to her face, her delicate fingers spread out on the pillow. Her blonde hair fanned out behind her, while several strands brushed over her cheek.

Most often when a werewolf spent time in their fur, running and living in the wild, they slept more than normal once returning to their skin.

How long were you in your fur, moon princess?

Slipping out of the t-shirt and boxers he'd donned to go downstairs, he moved to the edge of the bed, watching her. The gentle rise and fall of her breasts, half covered by the blankets, stirred the beast within him.

It had taken serious effort not to attack her earlier. He'd wanted to plow into her, not showing any mercy. The desire to allow the change had almost overwhelmed him. Her sultry little body had cried out to the creature that was part of his soul. His blood had burned to mate with her on the most primitive of levels. But sex in its purest form, raw, carnal, might have startled her. He'd endured the pain of holding back.

Trying not to uncover her, he adjusted the blankets, sliding in next to her warmth. Just feeling her silky heat washing through him made his cock burn. When she'd fallen asleep earlier, he'd lain next to her, holding her, while a fever had rushed over him.

Pack business had put his thoughts in order. Focusing on business kept him sane. But right now, he wanted to focus on Elsa.

She curled into him, turning her body so long waves of blonde silk glided over his arm. Her full round breasts pressed against his chest when she cuddled into him, murmuring softly in her sleep. Already the bruise on her face began to fade. Werewolves mended faster than humans, but he wouldn't deny the surge of pride that his moon princess had what it took to become queen bitch. His queen bitch.

Every muscle in his body tightened. Closing his eyes, he willed himself to relax, hold her, cherish her beauty while she slept. A fire rushed over him, thoughts of burying himself deep inside her tight little pussy overwhelming him. Never had he craved a woman so desperately.

Gentle and delicate, yet full of mystery, she'd entered his life needing protection. Little had he known how much he needed her. A figment of perfection thrown into his world. A world that was slowly turning upside down on him.

Elsa stretched, moving her legs so they intertwined with his. The moisture between her legs glided over him, the intense heat scalding his senses. His cock throbbed, bobbing between them, causing her to stir more. With the slightest of movement, he could adjust her, pull her to him enough to allow him entrance. Pain surged through him with the need to fuck her. More than anything, he wanted to fill her, hear her cry his name.

She mumbled something unintelligible, shifting so he could see the delicate features of her face. Those full lips parting ever so slightly while she whispered her dreams to him.

"Moon princess." He barely whispered, but pleasure rippled through him when her mouth twitched, a small smile appearing.

He couldn't help himself.

His cock pressed into the heat of her skin when he lowered himself over her, brushing his lips against hers. She responded, opening to him. The gentle touch of her fingers, when they glided over his shoulder, sent chills through his overheated body.

"Rick," she whispered, her voice husky with sleep. "Make love to me."

Nothing else mattered in his world. Her soft touch, the gentle caress of her words over his tortured senses, the softness of her body pressed against his were all that mattered.

He deepened the kiss, tasting the sweetness she offered him. Her tongue danced eagerly with his, her body coming to life. Gliding her leg up his, the smoothness of her skin torturing him further, she adjusted her hips, offering herself to him.

Heat wrapped around his cock, her pussy soaking his shaft when she rubbed against him.

"You don't know how badly I need you." His confession brought her to life.

She pressed into him, rolling him to his back. Climbing onto him, she adjusted her pussy over his cock, her fire searing through him. Her smile fogged his senses. She appeared a vision of perfection. Her blonde hair streamed around her, falling over her breasts, past her shoulders, fanning around her like a cloak. Sapphire eyes glowed while watching him. The way her lips curved into a luscious smile, satisfaction at taking control making her glow, made her even more beautiful.

"Tell me how badly you need me." She grinned, triumphant, while sliding her tight pussy over his shaft.

"Dear God." He would drown in what she offered him.

The tightness of her cunt, her moist muscles strangling the life from him, made him her willing victim.

She cried out. As he watched, her head fell back, her eyes fluttered shut, she impaled herself with his cock. He searched for words to let her know how he felt. But her beauty, her desire to make him her prey, her willingness to fuck him when he needed her so desperately, overwhelmed him, making it hard to form words.

Her long lashes parted, her gaze seductive. "Tell me, wolf-man."

She raised her hips over him, her tight pussy gliding over his cock. Lowering herself again, she began riding him, while he balanced her, holding on to the soft roundness of her thighs.

Her actions would make him crazy, send him over the edge. The slowness of her motions was enough to boil his blood. The creature deep within him, the predator who would dominate, fought within him. His adorable moon princess would be the end of him.

"I want you badly enough never to let you go." He tightened his grip on her, thrusting up.

"Oh." Her lips formed the most adorable circle when she cried out.

He thrust again, deeper, harder, watching her skin flush, her breath catch while he drove deep inside her.

Pressing further, her heat engulfed him, spreading through him, urging him on. He would devour her, take her over the edge with him.

The way her breasts bounced while he thrust upwards captivated him. Pushing upwards, gliding in and out of her soaked cunt, he watched her perky brown nipples. They were so hard, her breasts so full.

She arched, her hands drifting over her flat belly, gliding over those full round breasts. He moved in and out of her, building momentum, pressure building deep within him while blood raced through his veins.

"Oh. Shit. God." Her cries fueled him, the urge to pound her with everything he had driving through him.

His cock swelled, taking over. There was no holding back. "I'm going to come, Elsa." He wanted to fill her with his seed. Make his mark so irreversible she would never leave him.

But she surprised him. Jumping off of him before he could grab her, Elsa grabbed ahold of his cock. Her small fingers wrapped around his shaft, squeezing the life from him. Her moist lips, her hot mouth covered his cock head, sucking.

"Dear God, woman!"

She drank from him, feeding on him. Once again, making him her prey. He could barely raise his head as she drained all he had to offer. Doing his best to watch her, moving strands of blonde hair so he could see that incredible mouth at work, those spunky blue eyes of hers danced at him. Triumph. She grinned, white cream covering her lips, and looked sexier than any woman he had ever seen before.

Chapter Sixteen

Heat flushed through Elsa, her pussy throbbing from the pounding he'd just given her. And she knew she must be grinning like a schoolgirl. The way he tasted, the tingling in her mouth from his cock, empowered her, making her want more.

Reaching for his cock, she lapped at it, enjoying the mixture of her cum and his.

"Enough, woman." Rick grabbed her under the arms, pulling her over him. "Now we talk."

"What do you want to talk about?" She glided over his body, allowing him to situate her so she draped over him.

The scent of their sex drifted in the air around them, the rich odors intoxicating her. The way Rick lay underneath her, powerful muscles pressing against her, those chocolate eyes gazing at her, made her feel special, wanted.

"Tell me about your pack. I want to know why you were running."

That was the last thing she expected him to say. Her breath caught in her throat, while she searched for the easiest way to tell him what he wanted to know. Nothing came to mind. The sordid truth was all she had to share.

Rolling off of him, and shoving her hair over her shoulder, she sat facing him. Something dark hovered in his gaze. A menacing truth hit her, bringing clarity to her fogged senses. Rick was pack leader. Power and domination were his way of life. He would take what he wanted, and discard what didn't matter to him. Pure alpha male — born and bred.

She needed to say something. "I told you I am running from my pack."

Her comment was hardly satisfactory. His look told her as much.

"And is anyone chasing you?" Even lying there, relaxed and satisfied, he looked dangerous. His penetrating gaze, the firm set of his jaw line, his expression calm, yet serious. He looked like he could spring without a moment's notice, taking action on anything she said.

"Not that I know of."

He watched her, weighing something. She sensed it. No hostility or anger floated around him. But she detected something. Her heart started to race.

"What do you know?" She couldn't figure it out, but the calmness around him bothered her. "Why did you bring all of this up?"

Rick sighed. Leaning forward, he took her arm, pulling her to him when she would have stood. "Tell me why you ran."

His tone left no room for argument.

Maybe she should cuddle into him, latching on to him while she whispered the sordid truth to him. But she couldn't explain everything to him like that. Not sure of how he would react, she needed space, wanted to see his expression while she shared the truth.

She hopped off the bed, the cold floor slapping against her feet. No matter how she organized the story in her head, she could think of no good way to start. Walking toward the bathroom door, and then turning, seeing him watch her, she knew all she could do was state the facts and pray he didn't put her out for it.

"I'm running from my pack because I didn't like the mates they chose for me." Her heart pounded in her chest, watching him digest what she'd just said.

Blood rushed through her so fast the room began to spin. Calm breaths did nothing to stop the ringing in her ears. His gaze darkened, while he moved slowly to the edge of the bed. Sitting on the edge of the bed, naked, his body firm, muscular, powerful, he watched her, his gaze never wavering.

"Mates?" His eyes grew so dark they were almost black. Hints of gold appeared, her only warning sign that emotions swarmed through him enough to stimulate the change.

"Yes." She choked on the one word. "You see…" It dawned on her that they faced each other naked, yet no sexual desire lingered in the air.

The predator sitting across from her on the edge of the bed, muscles appearing a bit larger than a moment before, filled the air with domination bordering on anger. She didn't know how to share her story without sending him into a pure rage.

"Yes?" He sounded a bit too calm. The calm before the storm.

"We are *lunewulf*, purebred. Our breed of werewolf is endangered. My grandmother, our pack leader, devised a pack law to insure our breed would survive." Just thinking about how warped Grandmother Rousseau's plan was turned her stomach. Sharing the information with Rick made her feel inadequate, less appealing.

Fighting for words to continue, she realized she paced, the room suddenly feeling too small. Rick stood, making her stop in her tracks, and walked naked to the windows, closing the blinds.

"Go on. Tell me about this pack law." He faced her, crossing his arms over his powerful chest, dark downy hair distracting her while she stared at his well-defined muscles.

She could turn and leave the room. He didn't have her trapped. But she didn't want to run from him. As much as she wished she could keep the terrible truth from him, the best thing to do would be just to say what he wanted to know. And pray he wouldn't be repulsed with her—with her breed.

"Pack law says that every female will have three mates. There will be three dens, the female providing cubs for each of her mates."

Fury poured out of him, the glint in his eyes making them glow. She took a step backward, in spite of knowing he wouldn't harm her.

"And you have three mates?" His words were garbled. He was fighting the change.

She nodded. "I haven't actually mated with any of them," she hurried on to say. "And that is why I ran. I wouldn't have any part of it."

There. The ugly truth was out. Straightening, she refused to look away from him, even though his gaze bordered on dangerous. Tension rippled through the room, a good part of it coming from her.

"Their names." Rick broke eye contact first, suddenly looking quite torn by the knowledge.

"What?" He wouldn't go seek each of them out and challenge them, would he?

"Tell me their names." His growl left no room for argument.

Swallowing, she wanted to ask what he would do with the information, but decided it best not to question him right now.

"George Ricard. Frederick Gambo. Johann Rousseau." The list where she had first seen those three names appeared in her mind. That day, so long ago, when she'd first learned of her three mates, seeming like yesterday.

Rick moved in on her, larger than life. Every instinct inside her screamed for her to run. But she didn't dare move. She wouldn't cower, wouldn't let him see her fear. There was nothing to fear. If he suddenly despised her because of something she had no control over, then she would leave his pack with her head held high. She had done nothing wrong.

His calloused fingers raked over her skin, barely touching her at first, then gripping her arms. He lifted her, pressing her against the wall behind her. She fought to control her breathing, her heart pounding so hard it hurt.

"Johann Rousseau?" His face was inches from hers. His breath fiery hot against her face. "Your last name is Rousseau."

"Rick. There are several dens with the name Rousseau. I guess we are related somehow…a distant cousin of sorts." His arms trembled, or maybe she was the one trembling. "I haven't mated with him, or any of them. You took my virginity. You know that."

He lowered her, slowly. "Yes. I know that."

Muscles twitched in his chest. The spiciness of anger radiating off of him made breathing difficult. He fought for control, the way he simply stood there, inches from her, holding her arms. She didn't understand what demon he fought. There was no reason to be this outraged. She had run. That in itself proved she wanted nothing to do with the matings or the pack law.

The phone rang downstairs. The extension next to the bed chimed in half a ring off. Once. Twice. Rick stood there, not moving.

"It could be important." She moved and he didn't stop her, walking around him to the phone.

Before she could pick it up and say hello, Rick headed to the bathroom. The water for the shower started a few seconds later.

Chapter Seventeen

Rick was unusually quiet the rest of the evening, and even the following day. Something she'd said disturbed him more than she'd anticipated, but he didn't appear willing to talk about it.

Not to mention the fact that phone calls and pack members stopping by made a private conversation impossible. After talking to Rocky on the phone, Elsa hurried to answer the door.

"Got your car ready." Lyle turned away, heading back to his truck.

"Thank you." She hurried out after him. "What do I owe you?"

But the older werewolf climbed into a truck with another werewolf she didn't recognize, and drove off. She stared at her car, backed into the driveway, with four new tires on it.

Rick bought me four new tires?

Walking around her car, admiring how much better it looked with new matching tires on it, she wondered at the man who continued to baffle her with his actions. Pack business had kept him fairly busy last night, but she'd noticed how preoccupied he'd been. Then this morning, like the other mornings, he'd been gone by the time she woke up.

And now she stared at four new tires, not a cheap gift. Maybe he regretted investing the money in her now that he knew three werewolves lay claim to her.

But I don't want any of them.

Did she want Rick? And what did it say about her if she wanted a werewolf after knowing him for only a few days, but turned down three werewolves she had known most of her life? *Maybe I just know a good thing when I see it.*

Grinning, she hurried back inside to grab her purse, deciding she would take her sharp-looking car for a ride.

The diner had its usual smell of an array of foods cooking. Rocky looked busy waiting on a den at one of the tables. A further glance around the room and she noticed Ramona sitting at a booth, a man she didn't know sitting across from her.

If you really want Rick, you will have to challenge her. She'd never challenged anyone in her life. Fighting another werewolf to the death, laying claim to the title that werewolf possessed, was an age-old tradition. The thought didn't appeal to Elsa, but questioning the tradition would do no good. Ramona held the title of queen bitch, and there was no other way to gain the right to mate with Rick.

Walking over to the counter, so she wouldn't look like a fool standing in the doorway, she wondered how someone challenged another werewolf. Sure she'd heard the gossip of challenges happening in other packs. The news flew quickly how the terrible fight would result in one of them dead. Details of the bloody battle lingered around the gossip pools for days.

No one ever mentioned how the challenge began. Did the two werewolves discuss it over coffee? She doubted it. Maybe one of them lay in wait until the other went on their nightly run. That might be a possibility. But she didn't even know where Ramona lived.

It wouldn't be that hard to find out. She glanced at Rocky, rushing to get orders back to the kitchen. *Ramona probably lives with Marty – they are of the same den.*

"Hello?" Samantha giggled. "Girl. You were out there. What were you thinking about?"

She had no idea when Samantha had sat down beside her. The realization that pondering the challenge had consumed her that much freaked her out. Her stomach knotted while heat flushed over her cheeks.

"I'm sorry. What did you say?" No way did she want to tell anyone where her thoughts had been. Not yet at least.

"All I said was you look lost in thought." Samantha looked pretty this morning with her light blonde hair gelled perfectly so strands of hair dipped over one eye. "I bet I know what you were thinking about. Or should I say who you were thinking about."

She grinned, hoping she appeared coy. "I'll never tell."

Samantha chuckled, then reached for the pot of coffee sitting in front of her. Offering Elsa a cup, her expression sobered. "I heard about what Ramona did to your tires."

Elsa shrugged. "They're fixed now."

Glancing past her, she watched Samantha look through the large window toward the parking lot. "That's good. She's a real bitch. You know she admitted doing it."

She wasn't sure she wanted to hear what gossip might be flying around about her. More than likely, the entire pack knew about her now. If she left, that would cause even more talk. Maybe it would be safer to stay, and lay her claim on Rick.

Maybe that's what your heart wants too.

The smell of sweet perfume filled the air around them. Samantha turned, curling her lip. Elsa didn't bother to look over her shoulder to see who stood behind her.

"I thought I made it clear that none of the bitches in my pack associate with this slut." Ramona's high pitch just about curdled Elsa's blood.

"I don't give a rat's ass what you want me to do." Samantha straightened her long, thin legs, looking ready to pounce off her stool on a moment's notice.

Ramona's heels clicked on the floor behind Elsa. She gripped her coffee cup, willing herself to remain calm. Fighting in public was so low class. But dammit if the urge to change just enough to swipe her claws across that woman's face didn't sound mighty appealing.

"You better be careful, Samantha." Ramona's hiss filled with pure venom. "You're a stray we were kind enough to let into our pack. But I can run you out of town if you start lingering with trash."

"You better move on then, so I'm not seen with any trash." Samantha wasn't going to back down. Her anger almost drowned out the smell of Ramona's nauseating perfume.

Ramona's chuckle sent icy chills down Elsa's spine.

"Keep talking to me like that, and I might think you want to challenge me." Ramona moved to the counter, leaning next to Elsa. "No one *else* in this pack has the nerve to do it." She reached out, brushing Elsa's hair behind her shoulder. "Or are you just passing through, enjoying a good fuck before you move on."

"Why you…" Samantha jumped up.

"Samantha, no." Elsa hurried to her feet too, needing the distraction so she wouldn't bite Ramona's fingers. "She isn't worth fighting with."

Samantha stopped, meeting her gaze, her expression softening with understanding. "You're right." She sat, crossing her arms over her chest.

"How dare you listen to her when you ignore me." Ramona's squealing tone had returned. She stomped her high heel on the tile. "She has no rank in this pack. I do. You better remember that, Samantha."

Elsa couldn't believe the stupidity this woman possessed. It took every bit of strength she possessed not to lay a hand on her and wring her puny neck.

"You disgrace your pack, Ramona." She whispered her words, knowing already they had drawn some attention to them. There were humans in the diner, although she hadn't checked to see where they sat. "How dare you carry on like this in public. Your rank should be honored. You have a duty to be an example to others, not humiliate them."

Ramona stared at her, not smiling. Her brown eyes looked smaller with the heavy black eye liner surrounding them. Without a word, she turned to leave the diner. But just when Elsa exhaled, wishing the whole ugly scene had never occurred, Ramona spun around, an evil glint in her gaze.

"I simply can't understand why your pack wants you back so bad." She took a step forward, strutting around Elsa instead of toward her. Eyeing her from head to toe, she licked her lips. "As ill-tempered as you are, I would think they would say good riddance."

She didn't say a word. Not a damn thing came to mind. Her heart began racing, a cold sweat breaking out under her sweatshirt. Ramona couldn't possibly know anything about her pack searching for her, could she?

"Your pack mates sure weren't happy to hear you were shacking up with our pack leader."

The room slowly began spinning around her. Ramona's laughter seemed to be coming from every direction. She reached out, grabbing the counter, needing its solidness to hold her up.

Terror gripped her, but she had to ask. "What pack mates?"

"Now, let me think." Ramona tapped her long pink fingernail against her lip, a sickening smile appearing. "Frederick and George. That's it. Have you ever fucked two werewolves at once, little bitch?"

Elsa's mouth went dry. Blood rushed through her while the urge to change and run as fast as she could consumed her.

Ramona's laughter filled the diner. She turned, once again headed toward the door. Opening it, she looked over her shoulder, appearing very satisfied with herself.

"Of course I told them you were here. I wouldn't be surprised if they are in town already, looking for you. And the reward money they have on your head. I'm going to be a very rich woman." Her perfume lingered when the door closed behind her.

The smell of it made Elsa's stomach turn.

"What was that all about?" She didn't realize Rocky stood next to Samantha until she turned, noticing the two of them watching her. Concern covered their faces.

"Nothing. Shit." She was going to be sick. "I need to go."

"Elsa. Wait."

But she couldn't wait. Her pack knew where she was. They wouldn't care about this pack, about who they stepped on to get to her. She had to get out of here. Now.

Chapter Eighteen

Rick didn't mind working with humans. They were a harmless lot really. Talking to the foreman at the lumberyard, listening to him laugh while he shared a story about his son, he realized how attached he'd become to this community.

Moving his pack wouldn't be easy. Not only would he have to reestablish contacts, gain a reputation in another community as a good carpenter, he would miss the camaraderie of this town.

The older human finished his tale, slapping Rick on the back. "Looks like they got your order loaded. We'll talk to you again real soon."

"Sure will." Rick headed toward his truck, the wood needed to build the back deck he'd been contracted to do over at the Olsen's loaded down in the back.

This job would take up most of the week, making it hard to search for a new location before the next pack meeting. But he needed the extra money. He'd spread word this morning over breakfast at the diner that they would more than likely have to pool together all of their savings. He knew Harry took it the hardest. The older guy had done well with the diner he'd bought right after the pack moved here. Rick hated the sad understanding in the old werewolf's eyes.

Loyalty to the pack came first. All werewolves understood that. But that didn't make some of his decisions any easier.

If dealing with Masterson breathing down his throat were the only thing on his mind, he might be able to focus a little bit better. He merged onto the highway, heading out toward the Olsen's. His conversation with Elsa last night distracted him more than he should allow, considering the peril of his pack at the moment.

But he couldn't get her words out of his head. His adorable moon princess had three mates. The thought of annihilating all three of them, making her his mate for life, more than appealed to him. And he had a right to know their names. But when she'd said Johann Rousseau, he'd seen blood.

Elsa didn't understand the need to control all that was around him. There would be no point in explaining the dominating instinct that made up his very nature. He wouldn't have her worry if she thought a threat existed to her happiness. Keeping her happy was his job. And one he planned on taking very seriously.

Remembering how that alpha male had strolled into his territory, a little too confident for his own good, Rick clenched the steering wheel. Johann Rousseau knew he had no claim to Elsa. The werewolf's pack laws held no jurisdiction in Rick's territory. But he'd strutted into town without a shred of worry in the air around him.

Rick had wanted the werewolf's throat when Elsa mentioned his name. But he had no cause to challenge the man. Elsa had been a virgin when she came to him, willing and of age. Very willing. He grinned, knowing he would fight for her whether it was merited or not.

His thoughts flipped from Masterson to Elsa throughout the afternoon while he started on the Olsen's deck. By late afternoon, he figured he would head back to town, needing to tend to a few pack matters before he headed home to his moon princess.

Sweat clung to him, even in the cooling late afternoon breeze. Sawdust covered his clothes. A shower would be nice. Elsa washing him sounded even better. He imagined her petite body, suds running over her firm breasts while she ran her fingers over his body. Remembering touching her, turning her so he could see that adorable ass, he reached down and rubbed his cock. Blood pumped through him, making him hard while he envisioned water streaming over her round curves. The softness of her skin under his touch, the warmth of her skin, made him ache to be inside her.

Pulling into the diner parking lot, he sat there for a moment, immediately noticing Elsa's car wasn't there. She would be at home, waiting for him, possibly even with a meal waiting. The only meal he wanted was that sexy naked body, spread out on his bed, eager for him. Maybe he should call her, let her know he would be there shortly.

"Rick." Marty hollered at him, pulling him from his thoughts.

The serious expression on the man's face alerted him.

"I was just about to call you." Marty looked like he'd just showered, his damp hair clinging to his head. "I ran by your house, but when no one was there, I thought I'd stop by here first."

No one was at his house. He wondered where Elsa was. "I'm headed that way. Figured I would check in with

Harry first. He's good on that computer, and we need to find some property to claim."

He also wanted to see who was out and about. But there was no reason to alert the young werewolf that he worried Masterson's pack may be sniffing around.

"It would be nice to get settled so I can look for work." Marty wasn't the only werewolf in his pack who was unemployed. Just another reason for Rick to act quickly. Every member of his pack relied on him.

The diner hummed with activity, several cubs pumping quarters into an old jukebox that thumped out a popular tune. Both Rocky and Harry worked the floor, hustling around tables, while customers chatted about the day's events.

"Hi, Rick. Hey, Marty." Samantha grinned at the two of them, silently toasting them with a beer bottle.

Adrenaline pumped through him when he realized Johann Rousseau leaned on the counter next to where Samantha sat, looking a bit too comfortable with his surroundings.

"Did you talk to Elsa? Is she calmed down now?" Samantha seemed oblivious to the tension he felt building around him.

"Calm her down?" he asked.

"Elsa?" Johann said at the same time.

He wanted to pounce on the cocky werewolf. The jerk came to full attention at the mention of her name. Rick imagined he'd been sitting here pumping Samantha with beer, just waiting for the right moment to bleed information from her so he could move in on his woman.

"Oh." Samantha glanced at Johann, then back toward him, looking confused. "Ramona got her all pissed off this morning. She said some pretty weird shit. I don't have a clue what she meant by any of it, and Elsa wouldn't explain. But she ran out of here in a panic."

Rage mixed with panic rushed through him with enough ferocity that his bones popped painfully, the change begging to come forth.

"Tell me exactly what Ramona said." He would love to hear that Elsa challenged Ramona while he was at work today.

"None of it made any sense." Samantha shrugged, worry contorting her pretty face. "Ramona said something about Elsa's pack members. She'd met them and told them Elsa was here. Then she mentioned a reward. She rambled on like a lunatic. But it sent Elsa into a rage. She flew out of here. I haven't seen her since."

Fuck. *Fuck. Fuck.* "Were there any names mentioned?"

Samantha shrugged, her gaze shifting from one of them to the other.

"Think, woman." Rick cringed when she cowered.

"George and somebody. I don't remember. I'm sorry, Rick."

Rick turned to Marty. "Go find your litter mate. Take her with you and track down the two men she mentioned. I want them under lock and key." He nodded to Johann. "You aren't going anywhere either."

"No." Johann stepped around Samantha. "I can help."

"I'm sure you would love to do that." The thought of the werewolf helping himself to Elsa was enough to make him want to rip the man's neck wide open.

"Maybe we should discuss this outside." The coolness in the man's voice made Rick's blood surge through him.

Never had the urge to kill surged through him with more force. One down and two to go. "No problem." He gestured toward the door.

Samantha was on her feet instantly. Marty turned to follow him. He stopped the man, putting his hand on his chest. "Go do what I told you to do. I'll handle this."

"Samantha." The young woman looked wide-eyed from him to Johann, obviously clueless about what was going on. "Go over to my house and call me when you get there. I want to know if Elsa is there or if her car is there."

She nodded, giving all of them one last glance before hurrying out the door.

There was no time to waste. Elsa had run. He was sure of it. And damned if he knew where she would have headed. If she ran this morning, her scent would barely be detectable. It would take a bit of wolf power to track her down. He would use his pack if needed. But first he needed to secure the area, and make sure the werewolves after her were detained.

Following Johann out the door, he sized the man up. Several inches shorter than he was, and with a smaller build, the werewolf must want Elsa mighty bad to challenge him. He wouldn't stand a chance.

Johann turned when they reached the edge of the building. "I don't want to fight you."

Rick was almost disappointed. "Why are you here?"

"I heard from some of your pack that a new bitch had arrived in town. The description matched Elsa's. She and I are from the same pack." Johann shrugged, his lack of fear in front of Rick annoying him. "I thought maybe if she had found a pack she liked, I might like it too."

"And you expect me to believe that?" It dawned on him that Johann might know he couldn't defeat him, so thought he would try to outsmart him. Well, it wouldn't work.

"I know Elsa is running. Our pack leader has gone insane. And what you believe or don't believe right now really doesn't matter."

Rick still itched to teach the werewolf some manners.

Johann studied him for a moment, probably determining how much longer he had to live.

"If members of my pack are here, I can find them faster than you can." For the first time, the werewolf relaxed, his shoulders rounding while he held up his hands in a gesture of surrender. "Look. Keep me with you. I'm not here to cause trouble. Let me prove that to you."

"You won't cause trouble." Rick could knock him to the ground, humble him just a bit. Thoughts of showing the werewolf how to respect a pack leader almost distracted him. He didn't have time though, although he itched to pound the man just once. "And I guarantee you won't get near Elsa."

The man showed some intelligence by not smiling. "I won't deny she is a hell of a catch. I've known her most of my life." Johann paused, squinting toward the parking lot. "If Elsa wants you, I will toast your mating."

Rick sighed, praying that she did. "There are a few matters to tend to first."

Chapter Nineteen

Elsa unbuckled the collar she had around her neck. Moist sweat underneath the leather clung to her skin. The small denim bag tied to the leather collar bulged with her clothes. It had bobbed against her chest for the past few hours while she ran, and she was more than glad to have it off of her.

The cold night air attacked her naked body, sweat clinging to her skin from having run through half the night.

"I wonder where the hell I am." She pulled her clothes out of the cloth bag quickly, knowing standing naked in an open field wasn't the smartest move, even if she didn't detect any humans in the area.

Leaving her car in Rick's driveway, and running in her fur had been a quick decision. Werewolves frowned on running before the sun went down. But she hadn't been thinking clearly. All she knew was that there was no way her pack would haul her home.

She had left her car at Rick's. Whether she'd thought about it at the time or not, she would have to go back to get it. That in itself told her she wanted to go back to Rick. She wanted him.

She buttoned her jeans, then slipped into her tennis shoes. A quiet country road spread out before her, angling off before it disappeared in the darkness. After walking along it for an hour or so, with no town in sight, she wondered who could own so much open land.

What a perfect haven this would be for werewolves.

An old home, appearing abandoned, spread out before her, its sprawling porches and many gables offering secrets of past lives. A rickety "for sale" sign had been stuck in the ground by the road. She doubted many people drove by to notice.

The front porch steps seemed not quite rotten, and she sat down on them, staring at the incredible night sky that spread out before her.

What a mess her life had become. And all because she wanted her freedom. But running like this wasn't being free. She didn't want to continue to dodge werewolves, desert a pack just when she'd grown attached.

"And that's what I've done." Not only did she care about Rick, but also she could become good friends with Rocky and Samantha.

But Ramona had ruined all of that for her.

"Or are you letting her ruin your life?" Leaning back on her elbows, she stared at the millions of stars in the heaven, while thoughts of the previous days consumed her. "How do I take control?"

That's what she needed to figure out. Rick would say to trust him. And she did. But if her pack came swarming around, they would bring trouble to his pack.

Rick would know she'd run by now. And he'd be furious. She imagined him turning the town upside down looking for her. He would be worried and grumpy by now. Not a werewolf to cross.

"But what do I do if I go back?" The answer to that question hit her before she'd finished talking to herself. "You will challenge Ramona. That's what you will do."

Yes. Dammit. She needed to challenge Ramona before her pack could find her. That way, she would be mated to Rick. Her pack couldn't touch her then.

But was that the only reason she wanted Rick?

No. Hell, no.

She glanced around, knowing no one was around her, then lay back on the old wooden steps. Pressing her hand against her belly, she savored the warmth of her own touch for a moment before sliding her fingers under her jeans.

She would challenge Ramona for Rick. The werewolf was worth fighting ten women over. Never before had she met a man like him. So tall and good-looking, a tough exterior with a passion underneath that couldn't be bridled. He'd held back when he fucked her, she realized that. And she wondered what kind of lover he would be if he ravished her without hesitating.

Running her fingers over the warm folds of her pussy, she parted the sensitive skin, rubbing herself until moisture coated her.

"Will you be rough with me, Rick Bolton?" The thought made her wild with lust.

Thrusting her fingers deep inside her pussy, her wetness wrapping around her hand, she could see him watching her. If she closed her eyes, his hands were on her. He would grab her, tearing her clothes from her.

"Yes. Oh yes." She fucked her pussy hard and deep. "Put me where you want me, Rick. Fuck me until I scream."

She loosened her jeans with her free hand, allowing room to move so she could push deeper. Rick's cock would press through her narrow hole, gliding against muscles and hitting points in her cunt that ached to be satisfied.

Maybe he would throw her onto the bed, or better yet, up against the wall. Her head fell back, while she imagined him pinning her, his large body pressing against hers. The animal in him would barely be contained.

She pushed her sweatshirt up, the night air teasing her aching breasts. Gliding her fingers over her skin, she continued to finger fuck herself while running her fingers around her hard nipple.

Rick would push her against the wall, her breasts smashed against its hardness. "Every bit of you belongs to me."

Yes. He would claim all of her. She ran her soaked fingers from her pussy down to her ass, imagining Rick's large calloused fingers teasing the small, puckered hole. A quickening tightened her womb while her temperature soared. She began panting, fucking both of her holes with her fingers while pinching her nipples.

"I want you, Rick." She cried out while small waves rippled through her.

She didn't move, lying there exposed to the chilly night air. Her hand brought her little satisfaction. Instead she had created a yearning, a craving to experience the real thing.

Rick. Nothing would be right until she was with him.

With a broken sigh she stood, adjusting her clothes. It would be daylight before she could make it back to Rick's pack. But she couldn't run in her fur when the sun was up, the risk of being spotted and generating fear was too high. A nap sounded good, but there was no time.

"I need to go home." She liked how that sounded.

Home. Yes, and back to Rick. The time had come to take on Ramona, and claim what she had decided would be hers.

Standing and stretching, she imagined the wrath she would face when she returned to Rick. All of his worry over her would turn into anger once he had her safe and back in his lair. She couldn't wait for the aggressive sex that would follow the thorough scolding she was sure to receive.

She shivered against the night air, while folding her clothes neatly and putting them back in the denim bag. Once again she buckled the collar around her neck, preparing for her journey back to Rick. Anticipation riddled through her bloodstream along with the change. Bones popped, altered, transforming her from woman to werewolf. Her heartbeat accelerated, muscles grew. She dropped on all fours, thriving on the power that surged through her.

With the speed inherent to her breeding, she tore across the countryside, heading south, back to the pack she would make her own. Back to Rick.

Several hours later, the sunrise burned her vision, and her muscles ached from fatigue. At this rate, she would need a good nap before challenging anyone. Maybe she hadn't planned this so well. Her mind seemed lost in a fog, thoughts of Rick and Ramona, her pack, and his pack, all muddling together.

At first she thought she imagined it, the smell of other werewolves drifting through the air. The ground vibrated from their running. Several at least appeared to be running at top speed, toward her. She slowed, testing the wind, searching for scents that would clue her in on their whereabouts.

Warning barks alerted her. She stopped and turned, searching the countryside until she spotted a werewolf moving toward her. Even in his fur, she recognized her pack mate, former pack mate that is, George Ricard.

Shit. Not like this. I need to get back to Rick.

George stopped too, glancing over his shoulder, but then giving her his attention, his tail wagging slowly, triumphantly.

I'm not going with you. She lowered her head, growling her warning.

George pounced on her, moving faster than she anticipated. His ferocious bark terrified her. Panic ripped through her, while his impact knocked the wind from her lungs. If she could get to her feet possibly she could outrun him. But he'd sent her rolling, and her head hit the ground.

He was on her before she could clear her thoughts. His heavy breathing in her face made her want to gag. Coughing and disoriented, she struggled underneath him.

Get off of me. Her howls didn't seem to faze him.

In a wave of fear, she realized he meant to mount her, fuck her right in the middle of the field. And she'd heard others. Was Frederick with him? Would the two of them claim her as their mate? Would they take turns fucking her until she couldn't move any longer? She would be at their mercy, theirs to do with as they pleased.

No. This can't be happening. She fought. Determination flooded through her. Her vision blurred and she couldn't tell what part of him was where. She couldn't get up, and George was on top of her. She struggled until she found flesh, and then bit down as hard as she could.

George howled, jumping back. She hurried to her feet, falling once before steadying herself. She needed to run. There was no time to fight. He lunged at her, tripping her, her jaw hitting the ground with a thud.

Then there were barks. More werewolves. *Shit!* She couldn't think straight, but instinct kicked in. All she needed to do was run.

Another werewolf pounced on her, making escape impossible. She didn't know Frederick as well. He was larger, heavier, and his stocky frame about crushed the life out of her.

A prodding by her tail alerted her. He meant to fuck her.

No! God. No! If she weren't so damned exhausted maybe she would have more strength. Tears welled in her eyes, the pressure building just underneath her tail. Frederick crushed her hips when he mounted her, his weight impossible to stand under. Falling to her side, she whimpered, wondering what she could have done to prevent this.

A horrendous growl tore through the air when something flew over her. She was too disoriented to understand what happened. It took her a couple of seconds before she realized Frederick was no longer on top of her. Struggling to her feet, she shook her head, working to clear the fog in her brain and clear her vision.

Oh shit! The largest black and tan werewolf she had ever seen in her life sent Frederick flying through the air. Teeth longer than her human hand flashed in the morning sunlight when he curled his lip, daring George to approach.

Rick! She began barking, thrilled to see him, and eager to help him fight all at the same time. He turned, rushing into her. Almost half his size, she doubted she would live through one round with him. But he wouldn't attack her. She had returned to him.

Jumping back quickly, she barked her confusion. But his warning growl silenced her. No sooner had he turned his back on George and Frederick then the two of them jumped him at the same time.

Rick! Watch out!

She didn't need to warn him. He turned, muscles rippling under his fur, and threw George across the meadow, her pack mate rolled several yards before gaining his balance. She sat, and then stood, knowing she needed to help him, but understanding his growl to mean she needed to stay out of this.

Frederick moved in low, latching on with razor sharp teeth. He connected. She feared the tightening of Rick's body was the reaction to the intense pain. But he didn't hesitate. There were no howls of agony. Rick twisted, opening his mouth wide enough she swore he could bite off Frederick's head.

His howl curdled her blood. Those dagger teeth of his ripped through Frederick like the werewolf was made out of paper. Instinctively she took a step backward, watching Rick throw Frederick with his mouth. The werewolf landed with a thud, quickly changing into his human form. He was dead.

Rick turned his attention to George. The werewolf gave her a quick glance and then took off running, obviously deciding she wasn't worth dying over. Rick made like he would chase the werewolf down, but didn't. Instead, he turned his attention to her, his golden brown eyes glowing with a mixture of fury and lust.

Chapter Twenty

He wanted to send her flying for scaring him to death. And at the same time, he wanted to cuddle her to him, make sure she was okay, and cherish her warmth next to his.

Terror streamed across her face. More than likely, she'd never seen someone killed before. Her glossy white coat was matted, mud strewn up her legs and patches of dirt caked to her chest. At least he hoped it was mud. She better not be hurt.

Her silver eyes were bloodshot. She looked about her nervously, meeting his gaze only for moments before checking her surroundings. She appeared jumpy, sitting then standing, then sitting again. It wouldn't surprise him if she were in a mild state of shock.

A simple collar hung around her neck, buckled in the front with a limp bag hanging from it, more than likely her clothes. If they were worth putting on, he'd be surprised. His moon princess was a wreck.

More than anything, he wanted to haul her home, lock the two of them in his room, and teach her a hard lesson in trust. Running off like she had, leaving him clueless to her whereabouts, would not happen again. Elsa needed to realize she risked her life, and freedom, more by leaving him, than if she'd stayed by his side.

You will swear to me never to do this again. Growling irritated the flesh wound on his chest, but he ignored it.

Pressing against Elsa, he savored her scent, rich and sweet. He ran his tongue over her coat. Too bad he didn't have time to give her a thorough bath. She tried to step to the side, her worried look telling him she knew she would answer to him later.

Good, moon princess. At least you realize you've made a mistake. He wouldn't let her move away from him. She was so much smaller than he was in werewolf form that he could almost walk over her. Finally she sat down, whimpering while she gave him quick, short licks.

Pressure instantly built in his cock. The desire to mate with her, fuck her silly right here in the field almost overtook his rational thought. Instinct ran strong through him. The whole world had a right to see that she belonged to him. No one would try to take her and live through the act.

But he had a rogue *lunewulf* to deal with. There was also the matter of removing the dead werewolf. It wouldn't do for humans to find a naked, battered body out in the middle of nowhere.

And he wouldn't rest until he knew her old pack accepted her as his mate. He took her collar in his teeth, wishing he had a leash to attach to it, insure she stayed with him. A gentle tug had her on her feet.

Stay with me, he commanded. His quick bark alerted her, and she fell into stride, running alongside him back toward town.

Her breeding gave her great speed, a speed he couldn't match, which was the only reason her old pack mates were able to run so far ahead of him before they stumbled across Elsa. But she must have been exhausted.

He found himself moving slower than he would have while she ran alongside him.

The first thing he needed to do was stop by the house, check for messages. Ramona needed to be tracked down. If there were any other *lunewulf* in town he wanted them detained. And although he wished he didn't need to give it attention at the moment, word was out that several of Masterson's pack had run through town the night before.

My pack will not be run out of town in the middle of the night. They would leave with dignity. And they would leave when he said.

They reached the spot where he had left his clothes. He straightened while the change moved through him, muscles contorting while bones shifted. Pain surged through his body from the wound he'd received from that *lunewulf*. Glancing down, he grimaced at the torn flesh. It would need some attention before he did anything else.

"How badly are you hurt?" He glanced up to see Elsa focusing on his chest, worry pursing her lips together.

Her creamy complexion was smeared with dirt. But her impressive body never looked better. A bruise was forming on her jaw, but otherwise she looked unharmed. His injury no longer distracted him, other parts of his body drawing his attention and he focused on Elsa.

"Remind me to buy a leash." He couldn't keep his distance, knowing they needed to get dressed, but savoring just a moment with the two of them naked.

She looked up at him surprised, while he rubbed her collar between his fingers. But then her gaze narrowed. Would she challenge him, try to defend her actions? His blood boiled at the thought. He would throw her down and fuck her silly if she did.

He unbuckled it for her, freeing the small garment bag that hung down her front.

"I needed a way to hold on to my clothes." She reached for his hand, her palm hot against his skin.

Her luscious blue eyes gazed up at him, tearing into his very soul. She watched him take her hand, and he about lost it when a small gasp escaped her lips when he nibbled on her fingers, tasting her flesh.

"Don't you ever run off on me again." Thoughts of chaining her to the bed for a few weeks danced through his mind.

"I won't. Don't worry." Her simple promise melted through him. "And you won't put me on a leash either."

His body temperature reached a dangerous level. Blood pumped straight to his cock. Her saucy expression, the way she cocked her head at him, and those adorable blue eyes, filling with passion while he watched, made him harder than a rock.

"I had planned on taking care of some unfinished business." He took a step forward, letting her feel how hard she had made him.

Her hand slipped between them, her fingers wrapping around his shaft. Every muscle in his body hardened when she began stroking him.

"Oh? What unfinished business is that?" She teased him. She knew damned good and well what matters still hadn't been dealt with.

"Moon princess. You better stop that, or prepare for the consequences." She made him crazy in the head. It was broad daylight out. And even though they were sheltered in the woods, this was public land. Anyone could be traipsing about.

"Fuck me, Rick Bolton. I want you right now." She leaned into him, squeezing his cock with her fingers.

Everything in his world disappeared except Elsa. The passion swimming in her sapphire orbs would be the end of him. He could do nothing but obey her command. And he found that rather amusing. Here he was, deciding how he would discipline her, letting her know who was in charge here. He had plans of showing her how to trust him. And he'd planned on fucking her so many times she would never want to leave him again. Well, maybe he would implement that last idea right now.

Gripping her hips, he lifted her, her body easily sliding up against his. She wrapped her other leg around him, and he wasn't a bit surprised to find her soaking wet and eager for his penetration.

His cock had come home. Sliding into her, moving deeper between those tight muscles. Feeling her moist heat saturate through him, he never wanted to leave this warm, cozy spot.

Her muscles tightened, threatening to milk the life right out of him. With her arms wrapped around his neck, she sat upright while he held her, staring him in the face. Her gaze never left his, her look intent while she focused on him.

Muscles parted while his cock burrowed deeper into her cunt. He reached a depth with her he knew he hadn't reached before. And watching her blue eyes darken, tiny silver specks highlighting the swirling lust he saw there, he knew she bordered on exploding in his arms. Her body quivered when he pulled back, tightening his grip on her hips to steady her.

Milky cream eased his path when he lifted her off of his cock, receding until just his cock head remained inside her.

"Who do you belong to?" he asked her, holding the position, ready to die if he couldn't bury himself deep inside her once again.

"You," she breathed.

And he slammed into her. Her howl would have alerted any hiker in the woods to come running. But at the moment, he didn't give a damn. They weren't in their fur, but two lovers escaping to enjoy a heated moment. He dared anyone to interrupt them.

Elsa arched her back, her head falling away from him while her long blonde hair floated around her back. The curve of her hips into that narrow waist, her taut belly, hard at the moment with every muscle clenching down on him, those full round breasts and perfectly shaped nipples that were hardened into little mounds, all of it provided a view to die for. And all of her belonged to him.

He slid out of her once more, wanting to see her arch again. She raised her head, meeting his gaze, knowing he would dive deep inside her pussy at any moment. Her lips parted, her hooded gaze so sultry, inflamed with lust.

Ravishing her cunt, he thrust with everything he had. Her eyes widened, her mouth opening in a silent scream while her body tightened, contorted, sweltering heat devouring his cock while she exploded in an orgasm so intense, he knew she'd never experienced anything like it before.

Knowing he had taken all from her, he moved quickly to come as well. With another quick thrust, he spilled his pent up anxiety, all of his frustrations, his worry and his love — yes, his love — deep inside of her.

Chapter Twenty-One

Every bit of energy had been drained from her body. She had no doubts about it. Allowing her head to fall onto Rick's shoulder, she feared she wouldn't be able to hold on to him. Rick must have sensed her condition because he tightened his grip on her, holding her close to him.

Never had she been more secure, a feeling of safety and happiness washing over her. His cock throbbed inside her, moving against the over-sensitive muscles that clung to him. The way he filled her, stretching her, joined to her, added to her sense of contentment. This was where he belonged, holding her, being part of her, his cock deep inside her. More than anything, she didn't want this moment to end.

"We need to get dressed, moon princess." His breath brushed over her shoulder, tickling her.

"I know." She still wasn't sure she could move.

But he was right. Not only was standing naked in the woods during broad daylight not a safe thing to do, there were matters to tend to. Unfinished business. She was so damned tired though, none of it seemed so important that it couldn't wait just a bit longer.

Rick slid out of her, leaving her empty and craving his cock all over again. Lowering her slowly, he continued to hold her when her feet touched the ground.

"I bet my clothes are filthy." She turned in his arms enough to see the crumpled denim bag lying on the ground, the collar next to it.

"Don't worry. We'll go to the house. No one will see you, and you can shower."

If only that were true. Rocky must have spotted them walking through the back yard. She hollered from the door to her cottage, and then trotted over, looking very excited to see them.

"Thank God you are okay." She paused when she got closer, her gaze turning worried. "You are okay, aren't you?"

"Rick needs your pack doctor." She wasn't sure she could tend to that flesh wound. If it weren't patched up right, it would leave a nasty scar.

"I'm fine." He placed his hand on her back, the heat from his touch rushing through her. "Go take your shower and don't worry about me."

She turned when they were in the kitchen, facing a worried Rocky. "Do as I say. Go get your pack doctor."

Rocky hurried out the back door before Rick could stop her.

"Are you going to counter every order I give?" He brushed his knuckles across her cheek, not looking that disappointed.

"Only when I need to."

A wave of disappointment surged through her when he didn't join her upstairs for a shower. By the time she had clean clothes on, she heard voices downstairs. Taking the stairs slowly, while she tried to identify the voices, awkwardness plunged through her. Her stomach twisted, an unpleasant chill brushing over her skin. But if she intended to make this her pack, she needed to get to know everyone.

You can't run forever. Sooner or later, you have to stand up and fight for what you want.

"It appears they are staying at the motel downtown." Marty quit talking when he saw her enter the kitchen.

He leaned against the counter, arms crossed, glancing from her to Rick, who sat at the table while Miranda, the older woman she remembered meeting when she helped whelp Julie's cub, wrapped gauze over his wound.

"He'll be good as new in just a few minutes." The woman's motherly smile calmed her nerves a bit.

"Miranda can always make it so there are no scars." Rocky sat across from Rick, and grinned when he scowled at her.

In spite of the light conversation there was an underlying tension in the air.

"Who is staying at the motel downtown?" She met Marty's gaze, but then he turned his attention to Rick.

No one answered so she walked over to start coffee, knowing she would need the whole pot if she were going to make it through even part of this day.

"Rick..." she began, unable to stand not being informed.

"Your old pack is reported to be staying at the motel." Rick's tone chilled the air.

She turned around, catching the hard look on his face. His gaze bristled with anger, while the spicy smell of it filtered through the air.

Even with his outraged stare pinned on her, looking like he could murder someone—hell, he already had—she couldn't help noticing how damned sexy he looked. He wouldn't be countered, any fool could see that. But his predatory look, a look that told her he would fight for what was his, turned her on more than she ever thought possible. Right there, in front of everyone, she felt her pussy moisten, need filling her to please and satisfy this werewolf who sat staring at her.

"Maybe if I go talk to them…"

"You aren't going anywhere near that pack."

"Hold still," Miranda scolded. "I'm almost done."

The older woman gave him a motherly swat, his visage softening briefly for her while he straightened, allowing her to properly fasten the bandage.

"If I talk to them," she paused when he shot his gaze at her, fierce and threatening. She drew in a breath. "Rick, I am the youngest of three in a den that Grandmother raised. Her ways aren't right. I don't condone them. But if I show her that I am happy, that I want to be here…"

Everyone turned their attention to her. She hadn't voiced her feelings about their pack yet. A slow smile spread across Rocky's face while she looked from Rick to her. Marty rocked up onto his toes, although his gaze was fixed on the floor and she couldn't see his expression. A wave of satisfaction floated around all of them. This was what they all wanted to hear. She had just told them, in not so many words, that she would be their new queen bitch.

Of course, she had to fight for that title.

The phone rang while the coffeemaker began sputtering to life behind her. She handed the phone to Rick, and then turned to the fragrant aroma that would be her life thread throughout the day.

"Yes." Rick didn't sound like he wanted to talk to anyone who might be calling. "What are you doing over there?"

Miranda muttered something about being done. Standing, Rick gestured for Marty to follow him and walked into the other room.

"You've chosen a wonderful werewolf." Miranda gave her a hug before turning to gather her herbs and bandages.

"I know." She returned the affectionate hug but her thoughts were on Rick.

He'd walked out of the room. And she couldn't help wonder who was on the phone.

"Like hell, you are bringing that werewolf over here." Rick exploded, his voice booming throughout the house. "Samantha, don't push me or I will restrict you as well."

Wandering into the living room, where Rick paced, looking like a wild animal that would pounce without warning, she paused. The aggression that swarmed around Marty and Rick was enough to make anyone hesitate before approaching them.

"Like hell he wants to help. Woman, he is using you."

She didn't like his tone. No matter how fierce he looked, she wouldn't fear him. Never would she let him see her cower in his presence. She had seen him kill, knew his aggression wouldn't be contained. But she was strong too. And if she were to be queen bitch, all of the women in this pack would be her concern. Samantha had approached him about something, and if she officially held the title, this would be something she would handle.

"What does she want?" Rick paused when she questioned him, as if just realizing she stood there.

His gaze floated over her, obviously still listening to some argument on the other end of the line. Although still angry, she noticed he couldn't look at her without being affected. *Well, good. Damned good.* She wouldn't use his desire for her. But she would make him see that she would share all matters of the pack with him.

"Okay. Come over. But one wrong move and he will die." Rick pushed the button on the phone, killing the line.

Thick eyelashes hooded his brooding gaze. He stared at her, chilled heat rushing through her when he approached.

"My moon princess needs a nap." He brushed his fingers over her cheek, resting his palm against her neck.

A hand strong enough to break bones, yet he touched her so gently at the moment, almost as if he viewed her fragile enough to break. And if she were more rested, she would love showing him just how not-fragile she was.

Something wasn't right here. She glanced from Marty to Rick, both of their expressions masked.

"May I speak with you alone for a minute?" She would get to the bottom of this.

"You only wish to be alone with me for a minute?" He followed her into his den, whispering over her shoulder.

His words floated around her, almost making her dizzy with a craving to touch him. She turned when they were alone, watching him shut the door behind him. Those milk chocolate eyes still harbored anger, but lust swarmed through his gaze as well. She could reach out, touch him anywhere. He would allow it, encourage it. Knowing that made it terribly hard to concentrate.

Her pussy swelled, the pressure beginning deep inside her, filling her the longer she simply stared at him.

Heat flushed through her, the urge to run her fingernails over his bare shoulders, just above his bandage, consuming her.

"What did you want to talk to me about?" He moved closer, just a step, but close enough to comb his fingers through her damp hair.

"What did Samantha want?"

He towered over her, his bare chest covered only by the fresh white bandages. Rippling muscles along with his all-male scent made her dizzy. Or maybe it was exhaustion. She wasn't sure. Maybe it was both.

"She is coming over with a friend of hers." He stroked her hair, kindling the fire inside her.

"Oh. Okay." She didn't understand why he sounded so calm about it now, when seconds ago he'd been so furious on the phone. "Why were you upset?"

Rick sighed. Pulling her into his arms, pressing her against his injured chest, he rested his chin on her head. At the same time, there was a knock on the front door.

Chapter Twenty-Two

He wanted to order her upstairs, force her out of sight so that the *lunewulf* couldn't see her. Samantha had repeated to him on the phone what the werewolf had told him yesterday. Johann sought out a new pack, wanted to help. Yeah, right. And he was born yesterday. Any werewolf who showed no interest when told Elsa was to be his mate needed to have his head examined.

Another fear nagged at him. One he didn't want to admit having, but it wouldn't go away. Elsa might be pleased to see her pack mate. Johann had mentioned knowing her most of her life, and supporting her decision to run. If the two of them were friends, he worried she declined the mating because of the other two. If she acted pleased to see the werewolf...

You'll kill him. And you know it.

"What did Samantha say to upset you?" She repeated the question, looking concerned.

He heard voices out in the living room, realizing Rocky or Marty had answered the door. Elsa looked beyond him, focusing on the closed den door. He loved the way she cocked her head when she wanted to hear better. Pale golden strands of hair drifted around her face, falling over the curve of her breast.

"It's who she has with her that bothers me." He grabbed the doorknob with more strength than necessary.

Dammit to hell if he didn't want to walk out there and punch that blond brute in the mouth.

"Who is with her?" Her confusion made her blue eyes sparkle.

Laughter burst out in the other room, fueling his aggravation. He opened the den door, the laughter ringing through, while Johann Rousseau's voice carried over the others.

"I swear it's all the truth." The werewolf had his pack in stitches. Just the reason to flatten the man to the ground.

Elsa moved to the door, but he turned, leading the way. There was no way she would enter that living room ahead of him. If that werewolf made one move toward her, there would be consequences. And his moon princess would not get caught in the crossfire.

He pinned the man with his gaze when he entered his living room. Sitting on his couch, his arms spread over the back, looking like welcomed company, Johann Rousseau smiled easily. Samantha sat next to him, more than infatuated with the man. The others also grinned, standing around casually, a party in his own living room that he hadn't arranged or desired.

Johann straightened, looking past him, his expression suddenly growing serious. "Elsa."

"Oh my God. Johann." Her surprised cry hit him like a punch in the gut.

Dammit, woman. Don't you dare act excited to see him.

Looking away from Johann long enough to see the delighted smile on his moon princess's face, blood rushed through him with the urge to stop her from going to the man. But when Johann stood, looking more than just a little thrilled to see her, he'd had more than he could handle.

Grabbing Elsa, he pulled her back. No way in hell would she get any closer to that *lunewulf*. More than anything, he wished she would just go upstairs. As soon as he could get matters under control here, he would join her. Spending the day in bed with her sounded a hell of a lot better than dealing with the ugly mess that seemed to be descending on his pack.

But every moment counted right now. Enjoying Elsa's body, or simply cuddling her into him for a long nap, simply wasn't an option right now. Eliminating this werewolf, who looked a bit too smug, could definitely become an option.

"It's okay, Rick." She grabbed his arm.

It took more strength than he thought he had at that moment not to pull his arm free from her. And unleashing his anger, allowing his desire to kill to take over, would end his worries about the werewolf. He would annihilate the man. But her calm innocence defied him. She didn't act like there was anything to worry about.

"I heard you were here." Johann walked around the coffee table, but stopped before getting within hand's reach of him. "How are you doing? Are you okay?"

Johann sensed his aggression, which was a damned good thing. He better keep his distance.

"I'm fine." His heart swelled when she slid her arm around his. "I've found a wonderful man, Johann. Have you met Rick?"

"Yes. We met the other day." His smile softened.

That better be a brotherly look. No matter Elsa's kindness toward him, he didn't like or trust the werewolf.

"I don't blame him for not telling you about me." Johann reached for his back pocket. "I found this just south of here. Then after chatting with a few of your pack members, I guessed you had joined this pack."

Johann held out the folded piece of paper. Elsa moved to take it, but with a quick glance she handed it to Rick.

"I've seen them. And I've been dodging every town I could because of them." She acted like the piece of paper might burn her.

Rick studied the picture of Elsa on the paper along with a simple message offering a reward for her whereabouts.

"I wouldn't be surprised if Ramona found one of these." He held the paper out so Marty could look at it. Rocky moved next to Marty, looking horrified when she squinted at the paper.

"She said something about reward money." Marty nodded, repulsion spreading across his face. "I'm sure she called them out of spite. I'm sorry, Elsa."

The phone rang. Elsa gave his arm a slight squeeze before leaving to go answer it. Maybe she wanted to show Johann how at home she was here. He watched her leave the room, her firm little ass swaying nicely. Turning, he met Johann's gaze.

She's mine.

Johann met his gaze for only a second, and then looked down. *Good. Show some damn respect.*

"Rick?" Elsa returned with the phone, sounding worried. "More of my pack members just arrived at the motel."

After chatting with Lyle on the phone, and hearing Marty's comments, he knew they had to act quickly to get this pack on the road.

"Let me go talk to them." Johann glanced at Samantha, who stood, glancing at each of them before moving to his side. "I can see that Elsa is happy here. I'll tell them to head home."

"That might work." Elsa ran her hand up his arm, her gentle touch drawing his attention.

Looking down into those deep blue eyes, glowing dark like sapphires, he saw pleading in her eyes. If she wanted him to accept Johann, he wasn't sure he could give her what she wanted. He didn't want the werewolf's help. The last thing he wanted to admit was that things might go easier if the man talked to the pack.

"I guess you can come with us." He sure as hell wouldn't let him talk to the *lunewulves* alone though.

Elsa wrapped her arms around his waist, her softness pressing against him. "Between the two of you, I know my pack will let me be now."

He couldn't stop every muscle inside him from tightening. And he knew she felt it. He wanted her to know that he could fight for her without any help. He didn't need this blond pretty boy to win the right to mate with Elsa. If she gave Johann any credit for her freedom, there would be trouble. Hell. He'd already claimed her. Tradition ran deep with werewolves. And as far as he was concerned, Elsa already belonged to him. Dealing with the matters at hand was just a technicality.

But he wouldn't wallow. He wouldn't beg for her to see that he had won the right to mate with her. Not in front of these werewolves. Not at all.

Elsa would be his. She already was his. But she would also see that he had the strength, and the know-how, to take care of her—in all areas.

"Good luck." She went up on tiptoe, leaning against him, her arms circling his neck.

"This matter will be over before the day is out." He didn't mind kissing her in front of everyone. Not one bit.

He pulled her even closer to him, enjoying the way her curves molded so nicely against him. Running his fingers through her hair, he felt her head fall back, saw her sultry blue eyes glazing over when she looked at him. Her full lips, barely parted, were so soft, so warm. He brushed his mouth over hers, tasting her, feeling her moist heat. Then deepening the kiss, her soft moan into his mouth almost made his head spin with need.

He ended the kiss, knowing the men in the room waited on him. But he took a moment to relish the soft features of her face. The way her lips puckered, warm, full and moist, her flushed cheeks, and long eyelashes fluttering over deep blue orbs, made her more than a vision of beauty. "Don't go anywhere."

Her gaze focused on him, a small smile appearing on her lips. "I have some matters to attend to myself."

Something changed in her expression. A hint of silver sparkled through those dark blue eyes. She looked tired, but he saw, and smelled, aggression trickle around her. If she planned on challenging Ramona, he would be there to see the fight. It was his right.

"Any matter you have will wait until I return." He thought he saw understanding. Looking up, noticing everyone watching them, he focused on Samantha, who had edged a bit closer to Johann. "You will stay here with

Elsa. Make sure she takes a nap. Rocky. You stay here too."

The women nodded. He wanted to place an army on her, insure his moon princess would be safe until he returned. But there was no army, just his small pack. Matters would have to be taken care of quickly. The sooner those *lunewulves* were out of town, the better.

Chapter Twenty-Three

Darkness had filled the room by the time Elsa woke up. A silent chill loomed around her. Untangling the covers, she stumbled out of bed and down the hall, coffee sounding real good.

"I haven't heard from them." Samantha joined her in the kitchen, worry etched in her expression.

"And we have no clue what is going on." Rocky plopped down at the kitchen table.

She combed her fingers through her hair as it took a minute for her thoughts to clear. "Rick has been gone all day?"

"None of them have come back." Samantha moved to the counter, leaning against it. "I don't have a good feeling about the *lunewulf* pack — no offense."

"None taken." She could see both of them had probably sat stewing about this all day while she napped. "Grandmother doesn't care about other's feelings. That's why I left."

"I don't blame you a bit for running." Rocky twisted one of her curls with her finger. "It took guts."

Samantha tapped the countertop with her fingernail, looking desperately like she wanted to say something.

"What is it?" Elsa finished getting the coffee going, then glanced from Samantha to Rocky.

"I used to be part of that pack." Samantha spoke so quietly that Elsa hardly heard her. "I mean, my mother's den was there."

"What happened?" Elsa got a pretty good idea what happened the second Samantha looked up at her with those pale brown eyes. Her complexion, so fair, just like Elsa's, and her almost white hair were strong characteristics of a *lunewulf*. But those eyes, as soft as a doe's, weren't *lunewulf*.

"My mother was a tramp." Samantha shrugged, like it meant nothing to her. "I don't really remember all of it. Maybe she wasn't sure if I was purebred or not until she birthed me. All I know is she sent me packing."

Elsa couldn't believe what she was hearing. "Your mother kicked you out?"

Samantha straightened, that tough girl look coming through. "I did okay. A few years ago I joined Rick's pack. He gives me my freedom, but claims me as part of the pack."

"That is how Rick is." Rocky watched the coffeepot, her expression strained. "He knows how to see if a person is good."

Rick would do that. She could see him giving Samantha rank of a widow, or an older female in a pack, just to make Samantha comfortable. That way, she wouldn't have to live with another family, or find a mate she didn't want. Young single females had such few rights. And Samantha probably did well with the freedom to live by herself, and not be judged a loose woman for it.

"Well it looks to me like you might have found a werewolf who interests you." She grinned, deciding to change the subject off of Samantha's past. If Samantha wanted to share more with her, she would. "And you don't need anyone's blessing to go after him."

"Johann?" Samantha tried to sound indifferent, but color flooded her cheeks, which flattered her appearance. "I would like it if you told me you approved."

Elsa understood. As queen bitch, she would have the right to approve, or disapprove of any mating. But she sensed something else. Samantha knew she and Johann knew each other. Maybe Samantha needed to hear that Elsa thought he was a good werewolf.

"I definitely approve of Johann. He is pure alpha male. And I'm sure if he wanted it, at some point, when Grandmother dies, he could be pack leader." What a mess of a pack he would have on his hands if he took on that title. "That is, if he wanted to do that."

Samantha grinned, obviously satisfied that she had Elsa's blessing to chase the werewolf.

The coffeemaker bubbled, the black brew slowly filling the glass pot. Just the rich aroma helped clear her head.

Sighing, Samantha began pacing behind her. Her edginess was contagious. Pulling down three mugs, Elsa poured coffee. Not knowing when Rick would be home would make this a very long night if he didn't show up soon. She imagined Rocky and Samantha were already nuts, sentenced to stay here while she slept. And there were things to do. Things she needed to handle on her own.

She passed around steaming cups of coffee. "Would you two show me where Ramona lives?"

Samantha grinned, mischief dancing in her eyes. Rocky looked over her cup, her brown eyes wide and unblinking.

"Sure. If you want." Rocky glanced to the back door, and then back at Elsa. "We're supposed to stay here, though."

True. Very true.

"I don't think Rick thought he would be gone this long." She wondered how mad he would be if he came home and found them gone. "And I'm rested now. I want to find Ramona."

Samantha's smile lit up her entire face. She rubbed her hands together. "Hot damn." Looking around, she hurried out of the room, then returned with her purse. "Let's go find the bitch."

Leaving the house, she wondered again what Rick's reaction would be to an empty house, if he returned any time soon. He would be worn out after dealing with her pack. More than likely, he would be grouchy and ready for a hot shower. The second he realized she wasn't there waiting on him, he would be outraged. She cringed at the thought.

When her car wouldn't start, she glanced at the two women sitting silently staring at her. "Do we have a long walk?"

Thoughts of Rick's reaction to her decision to leave plagued her while the three of them walked along the quiet street. Something in her gut told her she should act on challenging Ramona and not put it off. She couldn't put her finger on it. It wasn't that she feared she would chicken out. It was more an impending doom that if she waited, she might be too late.

Either way, Rick wouldn't be happy. Those dark brown eyes, swarming with emotions, haunted her. Although pushing his temper should make her nervous, a flutter of excitement settled in her stomach when she thought about his reaction when he saw her. Mildly put, he would be irritated with her disobedience.

Imagining him towering over her, his dark brooding gaze full of reprimand, made the chill in the night air seem to disappear. Warmth flooded through her while they walked in silence, her thoughts lost on the sexy pack leader she was out to claim.

She clamped her hands into fists, able to feel the solid hardness of his skin under her fingertips. The heat from his body, his powerful bulging muscles. Thoughts of how he might take her by the arm, guiding her firmly to the bedroom where they could be alone to discuss matters, brought her body temperature to dangerous levels.

He could talk all he wanted. What she was doing needed to be done, and when she saw him next, she had every intention of acting on her right as queen bitch. Rick might be injured, but she doubted he would want gentle. And she wanted it rough.

Maybe he would push her toward the bed, preaching how she would obey him. She didn't know whether she would like it better if he ripped her clothes from her body, or if she stripped in front of him. But she let her thoughts linger to the two of them naked, his hands on her.

Her breasts swelled under her shirt, her nipples hardening painfully while she imagined him gripping her, sucking and nibbling on her nipples. Her pussy swelled, anticipation rushing through her. She wanted to ride his cock, force his penetration. Her womb quickened at the thought. Painful pressure was building in her at the thought of him impaling her, while she came all over him.

"Marty and Ramona live just around the corner." Rocky pulled her out of her thoughts.

The cold night air suddenly rushed over her, soothing her feverish insides. Her longing for Rick fueled her, while she studied the houses around them.

"Her car is gone." Samantha pointed to one of the houses. "It's this one, right here."

The simple, light blue, wooden one story home, sat in the darkness, giving no indication that anyone was home. While Samantha and Rocky hesitated by the street, she walked up to the door, and knocked on it.

"Well, hell." She turned after a minute when no one answered, the two women watched her in the darkness. "I wonder where she went."

Chapter Twenty-Four

Rick couldn't believe the chaos that had descended on the small motel. He doubted the management knew what to make of it all either. And as much as he wanted to go home, call it a day, and wrap himself around Elsa, he wouldn't leave until he knew all matters were settled.

"It's almost midnight." Marty stood next to him, his arms crossed, while he watched the people in the lobby.

Grandmother Rousseau, a small woman who looked older than the hills, moved slowly across the open area. Two men, younger than she was, but still quite old, walked alongside her carrying luggage. She paused at the glass doors, pinning him with an icy stare.

"Good riddance," he mumbled, still amazed that a woman could have as cold of a heart as that one did.

"Do you want us to follow them out of town?" Marty still radiated anger.

He didn't blame the guy any more than he blamed Elsa for running from her pack. The *lunewulf* had no concern for her other than her purebred pedigree. She was no more than a bitch to breed for them.

"I think we can give them an escort to the interstate." He would like to give them an escort clear back to Canada.

"I'll arrange a posse." Marty took long strides across the lobby, leaving through the same glass doors the *lunewulf* pack leader had.

Rick was charged with energy. It surged through his blood as well. The physical ache to take this demented pack down, challenge each and every one of them until they begged for forgiveness for hunting Elsa, made it a challenge to keep the beast within him at bay.

Glancing at the wall clock hanging behind the counter, he wondered if things might be settled enough for him to check in on Elsa. Her sapphire eyes would glow when he told her that her grandmother acknowledged their mating. Of course he wouldn't tell her the exact words the old bitch had used. Her hostility and narrow-mindedness didn't matter. And never again would Elsa have to endure them. She was free of her pack, and she was his.

Taking one last glance around the place, making sure all the *lunewulf* pack members were gone, he headed toward his truck. He hoped Elsa had slept most of the day. He had some energy to burn, and he knew just how he wanted to burn it.

Thoughts of plunging into his moon princess's hot little pussy, sucking her sweet nipples into hardened nubs, had him hard as a rock instantly. Need washed over him so quickly he almost couldn't move. Damn. He needed to fuck her, and soon.

She would be full of questions when he walked through the door. But her curiosity would wait. The second the other women left, he would take her. Let her ask her questions, berate him for keeping her in the dark. It wouldn't surprise him a bit if she were a bit upset.

He grinned, envisioning grabbing her shirt while she demanded answers. Those blue eyes would open wide, sparkling with energy. And he had every intention of putting that energy to good use.

Reaching his truck, he wondered if he would be able to sit down to drive. His cock burned to dive inside her tight cunt. Pressure built inside him, blood rushing through him at a dangerous rate. Squeezing his eyes shut for a moment, he focused on the cool night air.

"Bolton."

He searched the dark parking lot, looking for who called him.

"Wait a minute." Johann Rousseau strolled toward him.

The sight of him made it real easy for the pressure to subside. His blood continued to boil though. Just now, it wasn't lust that he felt.

"You didn't leave with your pack?" The werewolf better have a damned good reason for staying.

Johann frowned, looking almost irritated. "I don't approve of their ways. I told you that I wanted to stay here. And I have something I wanted to talk to you about."

"What's that?"

From behind him, someone else approached. A young woman, wearing a black leather jacket and tight fitting jeans, sauntered up toward them. The breeze caught her pale blonde hair, brushing it around her shoulders. At first glance, he thought maybe this woman was a relation to Elsa, possibly from the same den. But as she neared, stopping when she reached Johann's side, he decided maybe she wasn't. Her expression was harder, her face painted with too much makeup. Pale blue eyes looked almost clear with heavy eyeliner surrounding them. She had a nice shape to her, but not his type.

"Hi, good-looking." She smiled easily. "Are you the one little Elsa managed to snag?"

"Simone." Johann's growl didn't sound friendly.

She glared at him. "You don't need to speak for me. I can ask permission all by myself."

Johann stiffened, looking ready to give her a good reprimand. She ignored him, holding her hand out in greeting.

"I'm Simone DeBeaux and I want to know if I can join your pack, too. Elsa can vouch for me. She and I grew up together."

Her hand was cool and bony. He shook it once then turned his attention to Johann. "How many of you are there?"

"Simone has a daughter." He looked around her. "Where is she?"

The woman gestured over her shoulder. "In the car." She smiled at Rick. "I should get back to her. But I hope it's okay if I stay."

She didn't wait for an answer, but turned and walked away, the sway of her hips almost exaggerated. He had a feeling she used that body to get what she wanted. Focusing on Johann, Rick watched him, waiting to see how much interest he showed in her.

"I'll get her a room at the Inn where I am." Johann seemed ready to take on responsibility for her. "She won't be trouble for you."

He hadn't worried that she would be. Grunting his approval, he turned toward his truck, more than ready to head home.

Toby's truck caught his attention. The young werewolf took a sharp turn into the parking lot, coming to a quick stop alongside the two of them.

"We got trouble, boss."

Dammit. He'd had his fill of trouble for quite a while.

The sun bordered the horizon when he pulled into his driveway. Grouchy, hungry and exhausted, he looked forward to a hot shower, and Elsa's soft naked body, eager and ready for him. Although he wondered at the moment if he had the strength to do much more than pull her into his arms, and keep her there while he slept.

They'd spent most of the evening chasing renegade werewolves out of his territory. Toby had reported members of Masterson's pack terrorizing some of the rural human homes. An action he'd like to think Masterson wouldn't approve of, since the werewolves were teenagers. But it proved that Ethan Masterson's pack knew this would be their new territory.

"Well, there you are." Elsa turned with a spatula in her hand when he entered his kitchen.

Rocky and Samantha sat with the new female Johann had brought to him. A very young cub sat on her lap. Handing the spatula to Miranda, who stood next to her, Elsa wiped her hands on her jeans and walked toward him.

He nodded to the other women, the smell of bacon tempting, but his bed sounded better. Being awake for a good twenty-four hours, half the time in his fur, the other half in his skin, would take its toll on the strongest of men. He headed for the stairs, his insides tightening, in spite of his exhaustion, when she followed him to their bedroom.

"Marty stopped by earlier." She closed the door behind them. "He told us how you talked to Grandmother Rousseau. I wish I could have been there to see that."

Events of the early evening almost blurred in his memory. Her pack was gone, but now he had other problems. Falling onto the bed, he grabbed Elsa when she crawled up next to him.

"You should sleep, wolf-man." Her grin made her deep blue eyes glow. "Let me undress you."

That sounded damned good to him. "I will never say no to that." Rolling onto his back, he enjoyed the soft curve of her ass when she bent over him to pull off his boots.

"I heard there were *lunewulves* swarming all over the motel and you rounded them all up and sent them home." Her voice hummed through him, melodic and sweet. "Marty said you wouldn't let any of them bully you. He said you had them running to their cars to get out of town."

Marty exaggerated just a bit. Her hands glided up his legs, reaching for the button on his fly. He would have to remember to thank Marty.

She turned while kneeling next to him, stealing his wonderful view of her adorable rear end. Her long blonde hair fell over her shoulder, sweeping around his face when she bent over to kiss him. Her small fingers undid his button then slid his zipper down. His vision blurred, her erotic beauty swimming before him. Even though he didn't want to exert the effort to lift his hips so she could slide his pants down his legs, his cock remained full of life.

Bending over him, she kissed the tip of his cock head. Her steamy breath brought him to a boiling point. "I'm not sure how I can repay you for the way you fought for me."

He knew exactly how she would pay him. His fingers tangled through her hair but his reflexes must have been off. While trying to hold her head in place, he simply held on when she raised his shirt, her hot little tongue tracing wicked paths up his chest.

"Get back down there." She blurred in front of him again, her luscious lips hot and wet when she kissed his mouth, his cheeks, his forehead.

"Make me," she teased him.

He would make her pay for that.

"I am making you."

Her laughter drifted around him, a seductive drug luring him to sleep. She wasn't playing fair.

"Sleep, my mate. And allow me the honor of claiming you."

What did she say?

He licked his lips, ready to demand an explanation. But her fingertips traced delicate paths over his temples, luring him into darkness.

Chapter Twenty-Five

"You're kidding me." Elsa sat at the diner, a sinking feeling settling in her stomach.

The day had flown by, a pool of frustration that seemed to grow bigger by the hour.

"We went over to her house." Rocky pulled out a chair, joining her and Simone at the table. "Marty was sleeping but she wasn't there."

"That's when I noticed how clean the bathroom was." Samantha paced behind Rocky, looking like she wanted to pounce on someone. "Elsa. That bathroom over there is always littered with all of her makeup crap."

"Shit." She watched Jere, Simone's daughter, rock back and forth in front of the jukebox. Nothing was working out right today. "I remember her mentioning reward money. Do you think she used it to leave town?"

"You know where that reward money came from, don't you?" Simone picked up a french fry from a plate they'd been sharing for the past half hour or so. "Grandmother Rousseau made a big deal out of it, the bitch."

"What are you talking about?" She studied her cousin, remembering more and more of her traits the longer the two of them were together. Simone managed to suck on the fry without messing up her glossy lipstick. She always looked perfect.

Simone lowered her voice, leaning forward, her musky perfume drifting around her. "That reward money is your inheritance. It's from the trust fund your parents left you."

Bile rose in her throat, the salty smell of the french fries suddenly repulsed her. Simone's pale blue eyes pinned her like a dagger to the heart. The compassion she saw in her old playmate's expression did nothing to soothe the fire that suddenly burned in her gut.

Grandmother Rousseau had done everything in her power to destroy Elsa's life. Just when she thought she had won, had overcome the old woman's hateful grasp, it dawned on her that her grandmother was having the last laugh.

Well, she wouldn't get away with it.

"We're going to tear this town apart and find that bitch." She needed air. Pushing her chair back, she stood up. Samantha almost bounced next to her. "Samantha and Rocky, you two check every means you can think of that Ramona would use to leave town. Ask around. Find out for sure if she is still here or not."

Simone stood also. "I want to help, too."

They dropped Jere off at Miranda's, the older woman more than willing to baby-sit so the two of them could search the town. But after an hour or so, Elsa worried she would never hold the rank of queen bitch. Rick had fought so hard for her, coming home exhausted but proud to call her his mate.

More than anything, she wanted to go to him, present herself as his queen bitch. She didn't see him as the type of werewolf who would be satisfied with their mating if it weren't completely legitimate. Of course she could live with him, share his bed, enjoy fucking him every night. The pack would listen to her, the women honor her, but everyone would know her place wasn't secure. And it never would be unless she could challenge Ramona.

Fucking bitch. Where the hell are you?

Nightfall settled around the town when she followed Simone back to the diner. Dragging her feet, her thoughts bordering on depression, she wasn't in the mood for the sympathy her friends would offer.

Simone nudged her with her elbow. "Is Johann making the moves on Samantha?"

"The second he arrived in town almost." She looked up to see Rocky and Samantha sitting with Johann in one of the booths.

"Hello, ladies." A man at the bar turned on his stool, giving both of them the once over. "Join me over here."

He acted like he had been waiting for them, although Elsa didn't remember having seen him before. Looking around the diner, no one else she knew, other than Rocky, Samantha and Johann, was here. More than likely, Marty and Rick, along with the other men in the pack, would still be sleeping, or just waking up.

"Now, why are you so important that we should sit with you?" Simone's coy response brought back memories of how terrible a flirt she was.

A skill she had never excelled in; she always got so tongue-tied. She glanced again at the man. Black hair, darker than a moonless sky, tapered around his face. Piercing blue eyes that looked like they missed nothing, glanced from her to Simone. She couldn't detect his mood, he appeared calm, his body relaxed. But something about the way he watched them, studying them, put her on edge.

His slow smile showed off his handsome features, although he wasn't as good-looking as Rick. "Because soon, I will be your new pack leader."

"What?" She couldn't believe he had the audacity to say such a thing.

Simone took her arm intending to guide her away from the pompous werewolf. Rocky caught her eye when she waved toward them, gesturing for them to join their table. Elsa noticed immediately a very worried expression on the young lady's face. Rocky said something to Johann, who turned, and then jumped from the booth.

"My pack is moving into this territory in a few days." He nodded toward the stools next to him. "Join me."

Johann stood in front of her before she realized he'd moved across the diner. He almost completely blocked her view of the werewolf.

"I don't believe we've met yet." Johann's chivalrous tone masked the tension that radiated from him. "I'm Johann Rousseau."

"Ethan Masterson." The other werewolf stood, his height and broad shoulders making him easy to see even though Johann blocked her from him.

"Does Rick know you are here?"

She stepped around Johann, but his arm moved, preventing her from stepping forward. Obviously Johann knew who this werewolf was. But there couldn't be any truth to the man's claim. She hadn't heard Rick mention him.

"I haven't seen him yet." Ethan's relaxed mood bothered her. "But I heard how he ran that Canadian pack out of town last night. I commend your leader."

Johann nodded, then turned, gesturing for her and Simone to head toward the booth where Samantha and Rocky sat waiting. He glanced back at the werewolf. "Well, I'm sure you are quite familiar with pack law concerning mingling with another leader's mate."

Ethan raised an eyebrow, glancing from her to Simone. "I haven't had the privilege of meeting Bolton's new mate."

"I'm Elsa, Rick's mate." She stepped around Johann, knowing he tried to protect her, but too curious about who this man was. If she needed his protection, then she would ask for it. "Are you here to see him?"

"So you're who all the talk is about." His seductive smile brought her pause. Those intense blue eyes and glossy, black hair made him quite appealing. More than likely, his good looks and charm made it easy for him to get what he wanted.

Well, if he wanted her, she would soon find out how well he handled rejection. "I'll let Rick know you're here."

She started toward the booth, ignoring him when she knew he continued to watch her. Johann moved behind them, his hand touching her elbow while he guided them toward the booth.

"I heard you were looking for Ramona Rothmeier."

She stopped, Johann almost bumping into her from behind. Turning, she studied the man who had sat on his stool again, his arms crossed over his chest, watching her.

"Do you know where she is?" Her heart beat in her chest so hard she could barely breathe.

Ethan smiled, standing again, and then walking toward all of them. "I've heard some rumors, yes."

She didn't know what to say. Someone spoke from behind her, Rocky, or maybe it was Samantha. Johann had moved again, trying to get her to sit in the booth. But she couldn't move. Ethan approached them, moving slowly, a relaxed expression making him easy to look at. He smiled, those blue eyes twinkling, as if he understood how desperately she needed to know where the queen bitch was.

All the emotions from everyone around her suddenly exploded like a tidal wave. Whatever barrier had held them back disappeared, maybe her fixation on this man's intense gaze, and his tempting hint at knowledge she had to have. But suddenly she smelled fear, anger, outrage, and frustration looming from her pack mates.

Looking away from the stranger, she saw Rocky sitting at the booth, her back to the wall. Samantha sat opposite of her, both women looking very upset.

They didn't like this man. Fear rushed through her at the thought he told the truth about moving his pack to this territory. Rick hadn't mentioned it to her, but in the short time they'd known each other, so many things had happened. Maybe his good looks made her want to believe he was a kind person. Or maybe she so desperately wanted to find Ramona that she grasped at anything, or anyone, who could help her.

Ethan pulled a chair from a nearby table, its scraping sound on the floor making her jump. Damn. Her nerves were frazzled. He sat down, straddling the chair backwards and resting his large forearms over the back of it.

"Just out of town, about twenty miles from here, there is a bed and breakfast." He focused on her, those dark blue eyes penetrating through her.

She held her breath, knowing she had to hear what he would say next.

"One of the pack members from the Canadian pack was spotted there with her earlier today."

Chapter Twenty-Six

"It could be a trap." Samantha shook her head, glancing over her shoulder toward the diner exit, before returning her gaze to Elsa. "You have no idea what that werewolf's motive is."

Johann had escorted Ethan Masterson from the diner, and Elsa knew Samantha itched to chase after him.

"There is only one way to find out." She had to check this bed and breakfast place out. "And if she is there, I need to hurry before she leaves."

"Maybe we should go get Rick first." Rocky still worried, the smell of the heavy emotion surrounding her.

Yeah. Rick would want her to tell him if she chased Ramona out of town. She didn't doubt that for a minute.

Something inside her wanted to return to Rick with the task already done, though. She wanted to present herself to him as his queen bitch. And if she went to him now, she would never see that fantasy out.

Showing him she could handle this matter, without his help in tracking Ramona, or arranging the challenge for her, meant more to her than upsetting Rick. After all, if she couldn't manage the challenge, how would she handle the role of queen bitch?

Simone snorted. "Don't worry, Rocky. Johann won't let her run on her own anyway. Why do you think he followed her all this way?"

Samantha gave her an odd look, but Elsa didn't have time to dispute Simone's comment. The woman had a point. There was a chance that Johann would try to stop her from pursuing Ramona.

"I'll be right back." She didn't wait for any of them to ask her where she was going, but headed toward the bathroom.

One of them would follow her at least. She didn't doubt that. But she wouldn't let Johann detain her, or any of them. Now was her chance to find Ramona, and she needed to move quickly.

Darting out the back exit, next to the bathroom, she paused only minutes to undress. She fastened her bundled clothes with her belt, and hung them around her neck as she hurried across the dark parking lot. Johann or Simone would be able to keep up with her. She couldn't hesitate. Any of the others wouldn't stand a chance against the speed of her breed.

There had been a sign for a bed and breakfast that she remembered when she drove into town. Running along the edge of the highway, it took her no time to get there. And she hadn't arrived too late. Parked outside the rambling old home were several cars, one of them with Canadian tags. Ramona had a lot of money now. It made sense that her pack wouldn't leave her alone.

Now what to do. She stalked the surroundings of the home, remaining in her fur. It would be pointless to change into her human form and knock on the door. This was hardly a social call.

I will sit and wait for you all night. But what if Ramona wasn't in there? They weren't so far from the Canadian border for it to be uncommon for Canadians to be here.

This car did have British Columbia tags, but she didn't recognize it.

Anticipation and worry swarmed through her while she sat among the trees, watching the house. Rick and the others would figure out where she was before long. Although she doubted Rick would stop her, she didn't want to see him until she had her title.

Knowing how upset he would be that she ran off alone sent chills through her. She shivered, picturing those intense eyes, his hard muscular body poised with anger. A quickening deep in her womb fluttered through her. Her pussy swelled, moisture dampening her fur. Shifting, thoughts of him finding her, stalking her, had her anxious to see him.

Slow deep breaths didn't calm her while she envisioned solid chest muscles, his body large and capable of so much damage. If she waited much longer and Ramona didn't surface, he would arrive to find her sitting here, alone out in the middle of nowhere.

He would take her home, arrange for others to locate Ramona. That wouldn't do at all. Just thinking about how he looked when she left him naked on his bed earlier had her so hot she couldn't sit still. Pacing didn't help either, walking built the pressure between her legs.

Just when she thought she would go crazy sitting here dreaming about fucking Rick, someone walked out of the house. She froze, unable to breathe, unwilling to blink, while Ramona and George Ricard appeared on the front porch.

The change rippled through her almost without instruction. Not once did she let Ramona out of her line of sight while her vision changed from the heightened night view of a werewolf, to the limited sight of a human. Standing, grabbing her clothes, she hopped into her jeans while Ramona and George walked to the car with the Canadian tags.

Moisture she hadn't noticed while in her fur, soaked through her shoes while she walked through the grass toward the parking lot.

"Ramona." She enjoyed the look of surprise that appeared on Ramona's face.

"What the hell are you doing here?" Ramona glanced around them, squinting at the darkness.

"I'm here to challenge you." She stopped at the edge of the car, the floodlight over the parking lot seeming to narrow the world to include just them.

The look of concern seemed only to last for a moment, then a slow malicious grin appeared. Ramona let her gaze travel slowly down Elsa. She placed her suitcase on the ground by the car, and took a step toward her. Elsa held her ground.

"You and what army?" She laughed, more like a high pitched cackle. Looking over her shoulder, she ran her fingernails down George's arm. "And does he get to watch?"

Elsa wasn't sure, but she thought George looked repulsed by her touch.

She smiled. "It should be you that is watching him. You know he's with you because you have my money."

"Your money?" Ramona found that quite humorous. Elsa wanted to scratch her eyes out. The woman cared about nothing. "George is with me because I'm a damned good fuck. But you were supposed to be his mate. Maybe he will want to fuck you before I kick your ass."

Elsa had never considered the option that she might not win the challenge. Glancing from Ramona to George, it dawned on her that she couldn't take both of them on. Why hadn't she considered the fact that they might not play by the rules?

George opened the car door and tossed the suitcases in the backseat. "She probably has her pack surrounding us." He glanced around nervously. "Take her over to the field across the highway, and I'll meet you over there."

He hopped into the driver's seat. The engine barely started before he gunned the accelerator and took off. Elsa prayed he'd left Ramona and had no intention of meeting them anywhere. One glance told her Ramona was considering the same possibility.

"Change, Ramona." Elsa pulled her sweatshirt over her head, adrenaline pumping through her.

Elsa turned and watched Ramona disappear in the shadows at the edge of the parking lot. Within seconds, she'd stripped out of her shoes and jeans and then took off running after her. Although dark, she could follow Ramona's scent.

Elsa hesitated, then slowed her pace. When Ramona quit running and turned to face her, long white teeth glowed in the dark, and she appeared to be laughing at Elsa. Ramona sauntered toward her like the confident slut that she was. Her silver and gray fur moved over her muscular body, and in wolf form she stood several inches taller than Elsa.

Elsa slowed down as well but didn't stop. She entered the open area and decided speed would be her best asset. She lunged at Ramona.

Elsa knew that Ramona was bigger than she was, but she filled her thoughts with the many ways the bitch had dishonored her pack. She thought about how Ramona prevented Marty from pursuing Rocky. She thought about how she'd disgraced the title of queen bitch. She thought about how Ramona had contacted Grandmother Rousseau and told her where she was. She thought about how the bitch took the inheritance Elsa's parents had left for her. Elsa let her fury flow with her thoughts as she flew through the air.

Ramona had size to her advantage, but Elsa had speed. She felt the length of her teeth as she opened her mouth wider than she ever could in her skin. She stretched the digits on her paws and felt her dagger-like claws spread across the coarse, thick hair on Ramona's back. She dug in with her claws and filled her mouth with fur as she scraped her teeth against Ramona's thick hide.

Ramona's scream echoed across the field, alerting all wildlife of the horrendous fight about to occur. Birds took to flight. Rabbits and squirrels scurried for safe haven. Furious growls filled the air and patches of earth flew in clumps around them. Nothing else mattered. This fight was to the death. There would be no mercy offered by either bitch. Neither would beg to live if her injuries grew unbearable. These rules were understood — they didn't need to be spoken. Both of them knew what they fought for — a freedom and way of life neither of them could have if the other lived. It had been this way always — the way of the werewolf.

Ramona managed to move from under Elsa. She threw Elsa off of her and then charged into her side. Elsa rolled across the ground and struggled to stand before Ramona could dig her teeth deep into her belly. Many of their injuries would heal within a day, but there were injuries that could drain the blood and cause death. Elsa howled when Ramona scraped her long, deadly claws down her side.

Elsa's gift of speed allowed her to dart several yards away to prevent Ramona from latching her jaws into Elsa's hide. Ramona's jaw made a loud clacking noise as she bit the air instead of Elsa's flesh. Elsa turned to face Ramona and shook her head to clear the pain from her fresh injuries.

Ramona growled fiercely, showing her teeth.

I'm sure you say that to all your challengers. Elsa leapt through the air, remotely aware of other werewolves approaching, as she landed half-on, half-off, Ramona. The bitch had attempted to sidestep the lunge, but didn't quite make it. *I'm faster than you are, my dear.*

Once again, Elsa tasted fur. But this time, blood also trickled past her teeth. The taste was sweet, the texture warm and thick.

Somewhere far away, Elsa heard Ramona scream. Her mind didn't focus on that. She remembered powerful arms around her, and wanted to be in those arms right now. Elsa felt her paws leave the ground as Ramona tried to shake her free, but she closed her eyes and focused on the den that would be hers, if she could complete her challenge. She worked her teeth further into Ramona's thick hide, and gagged as fur and blood choked her.

Ramona shook violently, in a desperate attempt to free herself of the attacker on her back. She ran forward and stopped quickly, catapulting Elsa over her. Elsa ripped flesh and fur with her teeth. She shook her head and gagged, working her long red tongue until hair and hide fell from her mouth. Elsa licked her jowls and swallowed blood, refocusing on her opponent.

Ramona staggered as she attempted to walk toward Elsa. Her coat clung to her, soaked in blood. Elsa needed to go for the neck—break it, or rip out the jugular—that would end this. She bared her bloody teeth and growled her warning that the end was near as Ramona struggled to remain standing.

I will end this quickly for you. I'm not evil and manipulative like you are.

Elsa aimed low, running with her belly close to the ground. Ramona tried to bat her away and Elsa felt dagger-like claws scrape her face. Her own blood blinded her, but her teeth met flesh. She clenched her jaw and felt the pop, as she tore through Ramona's neck. The scream that filled the air let her know victory was hers. She could taste it as she drank the blood that rushed over her tongue and saturated her throat. Thick and sweet—it empowered her to do what needed to be done. She gave one violent shake and then shoved Ramona away from her.

Elsa staggered as she fell sideways. Dirt and blood made a thick paste in her mouth and she rubbed her paws over her face so she could see. Ramona fell backwards and struggled to get up. Her neck was torn open and clumps of red flesh hung down to her chest. The struggle lasted only for a few moments and then Ramona fell to her side, her head the last part of her to hit the ground. Her body grew still and slowly changed to skin, until a naked woman, torn and bloody, lay in the meadow with a dozen or so werewolves staring at her.

Elsa stared at the dead woman, feeling and thinking nothing for a minute or two. She'd never killed anyone before, and she waited patiently for whatever emotions would plague her. She didn't look away until movement from her peripheral vision caught her attention.

Turning her head slowly, her vision blurred. Was it Rocky? Who was the other werewolf? There were a couple of others. She didn't know them in their fur. She could smell admiration, a tangy scent, and looked at the handful of bitches curiously.

Rocky smiled and licked Elsa's face. Elsa closed her eyes and allowed the friendly gesture. It felt so soothing. She opened her eyes slowly when Rocky pulled away, then stood quickly when Rocky lay in front of her and then rolled over and showed her belly. The other bitches followed suit. She was queen bitch, and they were showing respect. Elsa let out a quiet yelp, letting them know that was enough, and they stood quickly and gathered around her, wagging their tails. Miranda and Rocky were on either side of her, and she realized she was leaning against Rocky for support.

Through blurred vision, she saw a handful of the male werewolves standing close by. A couple of them began dragging Ramona away. Her body would be burned, a proper burial ceremony for a werewolf. She struggled to stand on her own and exerted a fair amount of effort to stagger over to them. Rick stood in the middle of them and watched her with his dark almond-shaped eyes. She smiled up at him and realized she must look quite the sight. She didn't lie down as much as fell before him, offering her belly.

Chapter Twenty-Seven

Elsa turned off the shower, wringing the water from her hair. Standing in front of the door length mirror, she studied herself. A small hairline scratch traveled down her waist under her arm, but it would be gone before the day was out. Otherwise, she had a few extra bruises. Turning around, taking in the narrow curve of her waist, the roundness of her rear end, and her full, perky breasts, she smiled.

Now if Rick would only come home.

Sunshine peaked through the windows in the bedroom. Grabbing her hairbrush, her stomach settled into knots while she began brushing the tangles from her damp hair. She hadn't seen Rick since he'd appeared in the field after the challenge.

At first, when she reached the house last night, she'd been so pumped with adrenaline that she'd paced, expecting him any minute. But when hours passed with no sign of him, her mood had changed, worry set in. She couldn't figure out where he might be.

The back door opened downstairs, and someone headed toward the stairs. She smelled him before she noticed the top of his head appear in the stairwell. Rick turned when he reached the top of the stairs, dark brooding eyes devouring her.

"My queen bitch." He walked toward her, his gaze consuming her nudity.

Heat soared through her, tingling sensations giving her goose bumps while she backed up in the doorway so he could enter the bedroom. "Where have you been?"

He dropped a bag on the dresser, nodding toward it. "Getting your inheritance money."

She couldn't believe it. When George took off, she'd assumed she would never see any of that money. All that had mattered at that point was her freedom, the freedom to choose her own path — and her own man.

He reached for her half-brushed hair, gathering it in his hand, twisting, pulling. Her cunt began throbbing, anticipation flushing through her. Moving toward the bed, he guided her alongside him.

"Is it true another pack is moving into this territory?" Her question brought him pause. But she had to know.

He stopped, still holding her hair, but not moving. She could barely turn her head, and grabbed his fist, which held fast at the nape of her neck, so she could see him. Rick didn't look at her, but focused on the bed. His expression lined with exhaustion and bordering on something a bit more carnal, made her heart race in her chest.

Without indication, he pushed her forward, releasing her hair, causing her to tumble onto the bed.

"Where did you hear about that?"

She scrambled to her knees while he began unbuttoning the buttons on his shirt. Powerful chest muscles appeared, downy chest hair clinging to him, spreading over his sexy torso. Whipping her hair behind her back, she concentrated on her breathing. Her heart pounded in her chest. Either he was in a foul mood, or simply tired, but he certainly didn't look worn out.

"No one told you that I met Ethan Masterson in the diner last night?" The look on his face told her he knew, but the information didn't sit well with him.

Scowling, he ripped his shirt free and tossed it to the ground. His brown eyes were black with need. Muscles bulged everywhere. Her insides danced at the sight of such raw strength. An ache that had been deep inside her since she'd come home last night intensified. Painful need rocked through her with enough force to take her breath away.

"I heard he told you how to find Ramona."

"Yes."

Rick sighed. "The werewolf is taking care of his pack, trying to find the best territory for them. He knows I don't have the wolf power to fight him."

Elsa knew how hard it was for Rick to admit he couldn't defeat the werewolf. "Whatever happens, we will handle it together."

"You didn't let me know you were going to challenge Ramona."

"I had to do that on my own." She prayed he would understand.

"You knew better than to take off after her alone." He slid his belt from the belt loops, wrapping it around his hands.

For a moment, she thought he meant to strike her with it. Watching his hands grip the leather, muscles in his forearms flexing, her mouth went dry.

"If I had waited, she would have been gone." Her timing had been just right. "I would have ended up chasing Ramona clear to British Columbia had I waited."

She exhaled in spite of herself when he tossed the belt to his side.

"I had the right to watch my moon princess claim her title." His voice deepened, emotion gripping his words.

Crawling on her knees toward him, the heat from his skin soaked through her palms when she ran them up his chest. His skin was so smooth, black downy chest hair tickled her palms. Running her hands over him, caressing his strength, she stared into that dark gaze of his.

"But you did see it all, didn't you?" She had a feeling he'd been there all along.

"Yes."

She grabbed his shoulders, pulling him toward her, wanting to kiss him, needing to show him what her title meant to her. Fighting for him, for her freedom to choose him, for the security of their pack, welled inside her, building along with the craving she had to feel him deep inside her.

"Kiss me, wolf-man." Running her hands over the bulging muscles in his shoulders, his hair tickled her fingers. She held his neck, gazing into those dark eyes while his lips brushed over hers.

So hot. His lips were soft, yet his kiss demanded. As she opened to him, his tongue speared through her, ravishing her mouth, tasting her. Her breath came in gasps. She wanted him to fuck her now. She swirled her tongue around his, moist heat flooding her senses. Her nipples hardened, aching for attention. Barely able to catch her breath, she ran her tongue over his teeth, tasting him, absorbing his power.

The muscles in his neck twitched underneath her grasp. He moved his hands, undoing his jeans. He continued to kiss her while he removed them, until she knew he stood over her, as naked as she was.

She barely had time to catch her breath when he pulled away. Grabbing her hair, he pushed her down, his sexual scent intoxicating her when she went to her knees.

"Suck my cock, woman." His growl riveted through her, the swelling heat in her pussy exploding into pools of lust at his command.

"Yes," she breathed. She'd wanted this, craved his aggression, knowing it would empower her.

Licking her lips, then tracing his bulging cock head with her tongue, she heard the groan that escaped him fueling her desire for him. Tasting him, pulling the massive head into her mouth, her lips stretched around him. He filled her, thrusting forward while she braced herself, wanting all of him in her mouth.

"That's it, baby. Take all of me." His baritone lingered above her, inspiring her to suck harder, lick faster, work his cock while it grew harder than steel in her mouth.

He spanked her rear end. Shocked, not ready for the act, she cried out, gagging on his size all at the same time. Her reaction seemed to make him grow larger.

"Damn, Elsa. That is so damned good."

When he spanked her again, the sting made her blood boil, her pussy swelled, moisture pooled between her legs.

"You took a hell of a risk last night." His words swam above her, filtering through her while she worked his cock.

The velvety skin over his rock-hard shaft moved against her tingling lips. Tasting the saltiness of him made her drunk with desire. She wanted more. Needed more. Craved every bit of him.

Another swat on her rear had her squirming, crying out while his cock moved in and out of her mouth. Pressure threatened to explode inside her. Thoughts of begging him to fuck her had her soaked.

Needing to catch her breath, she gripped his shaft, allowing him to slide from her mouth.

"The risk was worth it." Her lips were swollen, making her words muffled.

He spanked her again, but this time she rolled over, holding on to his cock, pulling him toward her.

Falling above her, his arms bracing him so that he hovered over her, he stared at her with a lust-filled gaze.

"You were two against one."

"And I managed just fine." Stroking him while she spoke, she loved watching his eyes half close while he fought to keep control. "Just as I will manage you, wolf-man."

His gaze darkened, piercing her with an intent that exhilarated her. Taking her hands from his cock, he pinned her wrists on either side of her head. "Who will manage whom?"

She smiled at his display of doubt that she would be able to control him. Twisting her wrists under his grasp, knowing she couldn't move unless he willed it, she stared up at him, her pussy dripping with cum.

"Already I have you doing exactly what I want you to do." She couldn't help herself, feeling high from the strength and domination that he exerted over her. Wrapping her legs around his waist, she willed his cock toward her pussy. "Fuck me, wolf-man."

He slammed so deep inside her with his first thrust that she wondered if he hadn't plowed right through her.

"Dear God," she cried out, more like screamed.

Pulling out slowly, he devoured her with his half opened eyes. Lowering his mouth to hers, he nibbled on her lip, biting at the same time that he dove deep inside her again.

"Rick." He had to be fucking her clear up to her belly button.

His movements increased, friction building against the heat between her thighs. Her body heat soared, her cum soaking her while he fucked her, claimed her. Tightening her legs around him, wanting him even deeper inside her, she knew he would take her over the edge, fuck her until she could no longer think, no longer breathe.

Pressure threatened to kill her if she didn't explode soon. She just knew it. And even though she held him to her, he managed to pull out, her body teetering on the edge of orgasm.

"Rick. What?" She didn't understand.

Unable to focus, she blinked, trying to catch her breath while she watched him kneel over her, holding his cock, stroking it slowly. The sight of her thick, white cum clinging to his shaft made her mouth water. She couldn't look away.

"What are you doing? You aren't done."

His grin had her gasping for breath. He had taken control, her body craving what only he could give her. No way could she make demands right now, more like beg like a babbling idiot if he didn't stick his cock back inside her soon.

He took her hand, his hand damp from her cum, and placed her fingers on her throbbing pussy.

"Fuck yourself, moon princess. I want to watch you masturbate."

The intensity of heat inside her cunt absorbed through her, when she slid her fingers inside, almost making her come right then. She couldn't breathe, gasping while she stared up at him. His attention was on her hand, and what she was doing to herself, while he slowly stroked that massive cock.

Getting into the act, feeling her power return now that she had captivated his attention, she squirmed in front of him, moving her hips while she finger fucked herself. She ran her other hand over her breast, squeezing her nipple, and then back to her pussy, watching him watch her. The groan that escaped him soaked her, her rich cream seeping down her ass.

Letting go of his cock, he spread her legs, changing how she felt inside. She began fucking herself faster, harder. His fingers joined hers, tracing paths around her pussy, spreading her cum over her ass.

"I'm going to fuck you here." His finger dipped inside her ass, the pressure not what she expected.

His finger matched the movement of hers. He fucked her ass while she fucked her pussy, the sensations that rippled through her bringing her so close to exploding she could feel it, but not quite get there.

"Rick. Please." She needed him. Needed more. Her body craving to experience what only he could give her.

"Please what, moon princess?" He was a blur above her, his voice a soothing tease that wrapped around her senses.

"Fuck me. Please, fuck me."

"I want to fuck your ass."

"Okay." Anywhere. Anything. He'd managed to capture complete control of her, but she no longer cared, just needing to explode.

"Tell me that you want me too." He'd pulled his finger from her ass, replacing it with the tip of his cock.

She could feel him press against her, her skin already stretching in an effort to wrap around him. Her fingers were so wet, the thick moisture soaking his cock, saturating around her ass.

"Fuck my ass, Rick. Please fuck my ass."

Pressure soared around her tender hole, heat rushing through her while the sensitive skin stretched. She absorbed him, feeling him fill her, pushing deep inside her.

"God. Rick. Oh my God." She bucked, not ready for the intensity of the invading pressure.

"Relax, baby. Take deep breaths and relax your body." This time, his voice soothed her, wrapping around her feverish skin.

Doing her best to do as he asked, she sucked in air, her fingers deep inside her pussy feeling his cock move in and out of her ass. Every nerve ending reacted to him. His cock flowed through her, then receded, gliding with more fluency than she imagined.

"You're so tight. So hot." He sounded tortured, his breath heavy. "I'm going to come, baby. I can't hold back any longer."

Without further warning, he spewed hot seed deep inside her ass, the sensation rippling through her. Exploding along with him, she opened her eyes, gasping, when he pulled out quickly, grabbing her wrist and freeing her hands from her pussy.

"Incredible, Rick. Absolutely incredible." She swore she floated.

He collapsed above her, crushing her momentarily before his strong arms wrapped around her and pulled her on top of him as he rolled over.

"I love you." He pinned her to him, his hand grasping the back of her head while he kissed her.

Out of breath, she gasped in his mouth, smiling, loving the feel of their bodies intertwined.

"I love you too, Rick." She'd found true happiness, in a life where she'd almost given up hope that such a thing existed. But here, with Rick, and her new pack, they would make their home, wherever that might be. She knew there would be no problems, just challenges that they would enjoy together.

The End

LUNEWULF 3: IN HER DREAMS

Lorie O'Clare

Preview

IN HER DREAMS

Elsa pulled into the gravel parking lot of the diner where most of the pack congregated by midday. Samantha glanced around at the lack of cars.

She felt more nervous than a trapped doe when they parked in front of Harry's diner. What would Johann think? Elsa had just purchased a boarding house with her inheritance money. Rick would move the pack immediately. She had no choice but to stay with her pack; she was a single bitch.

But Johann...She wanted to be with Johann. Would he move with the pack?

"Closed?" Samantha stared at the sign hanging crooked on the glass door to the establishment. "Why would they be closed?"

"When was the last time the diner closed?" Elsa's bewilderment filled the air around them.

"It's open twenty-four hours, in case anyone wants to stop in after a run." Samantha peered through the glass, staring at the empty tables inside. "This doesn't make sense."

She turned to stare at Elsa. "I wonder where Johann is."

They both turned at the sound of popping gravel. Simone DeBeaux, the *Lunewulf* bitch who'd joined the pack when Johann had, pulled to a stop in front of them, dust from the gravel filling the air.

She rolled down her window, lifted her sunglasses and squinted at them. "Johann sent me to look for you. Everyone is over at Miranda's. Better hurry."

Her tone left no room for argument. She let her glasses drop over her nose and brushed her hair with her fingers while she drove off. Samantha stared after her, unable to stop the twinge of jealousy that ran through her. Simone had known Johann from their previous pack, both of them being *Lunewulf*. And even though Johann ignored Simone for the most part, the two of them had a cub together. She knew Johann well enough to know he would look out for his den, legitimate or not.

"Johann doesn't want her. Trust me." Elsa squeezed Samantha's arm.

She turned to search Elsa's concerned expression. "We better go find out what is going on."

Minutes later they entered through the back door at Miranda's. The smell of anger and pain flooded Samantha's senses, tying her stomach in knots. Something was wrong. Terribly wrong.

"There you are." Miranda looked up from a salve she stirred in a wooden bowl.

"I had some business to take care of. What are you making?" Elsa wrinkled her brow as she sniffed the air. "Is someone hurt?"

"You've missed some excitement." Miranda nodded toward her living room and carried the bowl in that direction.

Samantha followed Miranda and Elsa into the living room and gasped at the makeshift hospital in front of her.

"What happened?" Elsa looked at Miranda, who began covering a rather deep gash on Lyle's arm with her pink-gray poultice.

"Two rogue werewolves did this. They thought they could enter town and find themselves a piece of tail." Lyle spoke through gritted teeth as he watched his arm being wrapped in gauze.

Miranda secured the gauze near her mate's elbow. "We thought they were from Ethan Masterson's pack, you know, trying to claim the territory. But he didn't know them. They went after Rocky."

"Holy shit! Was she hurt?" Samantha looked around the room for her friend.

Elsa started helping Miranda, immediately assuming the role of queen bitch. But Samantha wanted to know where everyone was, where Johann was.

"Rocky got a little beat up I'm told. Marty is bringing her over, although I hardly know where to put them." Miranda looked around at her three patients. "I can only tend to them so fast. I guess we can put her in one of the bedrooms upstairs."

Elsa shook her head. "Let's take her over to Rick's house. There is plenty of room there."

"Where did this happen?" Samantha watched while Miranda gathered several herbs to send with Elsa.

"At the diner. Harry had to close the place. I guess Rocky was sitting at the counter and Harry was back in his office. He tried to stop the two men when they decided to help themselves to things that weren't on the menu." Once she was satisfied with the medicinal supplies to be sent with Elsa, Miranda reached for her phone. "You might as well head on out. I'll call Marty and have him tell Rick that his queen bitch is executing her rights."

Samantha chewed her lip all the way over to Rick's. She wondered where Johann was. He would go after those two rogues. No matter what Rick ordered. Johann would take matters into his own hands. But what if there were others? A sick feeling rose in her stomach at the thought of Johann getting hurt. With a new pack moving in, werewolves would test their boundaries, disregard pack leaders' orders. Anything could happen.

"Why don't you go find Johann?" Elsa patted her arm after they parked in Rick's driveway. "You'll feel much better after you do."

Samantha smiled, but she couldn't stop the dread that grew in her gut. Uneasiness rolled in the air around them. Bad times lay ahead.

About the author:

All my life, I've wondered at how people fall into the routines of life. The paths we travel seemed to be well-trodden by society. We go to school, fall in love, find a line of work (and hope and pray it is one we like), have children and do our best to mold them into good people who will travel the same path. This is the path so commonly referred to as the "real world".

The characters in my books are destined to stray down a different path other than the one society suggests. Each story leads the reader into a world altered slightly from the one they know. For me, this is what good fiction is about, an opportunity to escape from the daily grind and wander down someone else's path.

Lorie O'Clare lives in Kansas with her three sons.

Lorie welcomes mail from readers. You can write to her c/o Ellora's Cave Publishing at 1337 Commerce Drive, Suite 13, Stow OH 44224.

Also by Lorie O'Clare:

Why an electronic book?

We live in the Information Age—an exciting time in the history of human civilization in which technology rules supreme and continues to progress in leaps and bounds every minute of every hour of every day. For a multitude of reasons, more and more avid literary fans are opting to purchase e-books instead of paperbacks. The question to those not yet initiated to the world of electronic reading is simply: *why?*

1. *Price.* An electronic title at Ellora's Cave Publishing runs anywhere from 40-75% less than the cover price of the <u>exact same title</u> in paperback format. Why? Cold mathematics. It is less expensive to publish an e-book than it is to publish a paperback, so the savings are passed along to the consumer.

2. *Space.* Running out of room to house your paperback books? That is one worry you will never have with electronic novels. For a low one-time cost, you can purchase a handheld computer designed specifically for e-reading purposes. Many e-readers are larger than the average handheld, giving you plenty of screen room. Better yet, hundreds of titles can be stored within your new library—a single microchip. (Please note that Ellora's Cave does not endorse any specific brands. You can check our website at www.ellorascave.com for customer

recommendations we make available to new consumers.)

3. *Mobility.* Because your new library now consists of only a microchip, your entire cache of books can be taken with you wherever you go.

4. *Personal preferences are accounted for.* Are the words you are currently reading too small? Too large? Too...**ANNOYING**? Paperback books cannot be modified according to personal preferences, but e-books can.

5. *Innovation.* The way you read a book is not the only advancement the Information Age has gifted the literary community with. There is also the factor of what you can read. Ellora's Cave Publishing will be introducing a new line of interactive titles that are available in e-book format only.

6. *Instant gratification.* Is it the middle of the night and all the bookstores are closed? Are you tired of waiting days—sometimes weeks—for online and offline bookstores to ship the novels you bought? Ellora's Cave Publishing sells instantaneous downloads 24 hours a day, 7 days a week, 365 days a year. Our e-book delivery system is 100% automated, meaning your order is filled as soon as you pay for it.

Those are a few of the top reasons why electronic novels are displacing paperbacks for many an avid reader. As always, Ellora's Cave Publishing welcomes your questions and comments. We invite you to email us at service@ellorascave.com or write to us directly at: 1337 Commerce Drive, Suite 13, Stow OH 44224.

Printed in the United States
39149LVS00001B/73-120